"I want someone entirely natural."

Paul waved her to a chair. "A woman with a dreamlike quality of innocence," he continued. "In short, I want the woman I met on the beach. If you can deliver that, the commercial is yours."

"You'd ask that of me?" Eve choked out.

Surprise flickered in his eyes. "Do you mean that afternoon meant something special to you?"

He'd made it impossible. "Only in so far as any fantasy is special," she replied carelessly.

"Ah, yes. Fantasy!" Paul's mouth curved with grim amusement. "That's the name we've chosen for our new perfume. I'm sure you'll do it justice. After all, you can make a fantasy . . . almost real."

Eve wanted to hurl his job offer in his face. Was he prepared to peddle her soul for a perfume?

EMMA DARCY

fantasy

Harlequin Books

TORONTO • NEW YORK • LONDON
AMSTERDAM • PARIS • SYDNEY • HAMBURG
STOCKHOLM • ATHENS • TOKYO • MILAN

Harlequin Presents first edition December 1985
Second printing January 1986
ISBN 0-373-10840-0

Original hardcover edition published in 1985
by Mills & Boon Limited

Printed in U.S.A.

CHAPTER ONE

THE car lurched from one pothole to the next. Steering a steady course was fast becoming impossible. Dense bush-scrub crowded in on the dirt track and just as Eve began to think she had made a mistake, it thinned out and there was the sea.

She brought the car to an abrupt halt. As she leant forward to switch off the headlights, another light seemed to wink at her from the darkness ahead. She closed her tired lids, squeezed some of the strain from her eyes, then looked again. Nothing. The darkness around her was complete. Relief poured its soothing oil on over-stretched nerves. She was alone. Not only alone but well away from any human contact. She could stay here without fear of anyone coming to question or look at her with curious eyes.

For a long, weary moment she rested her head on the car-door. The tangy crispness of sea air drifted through the open window and teased her nostrils. It smelled clean. The peaceful drone of lapping waves washed through her fretful mind. Eve did not want to think any more. Every thought brought a bitter sickness. As another shudder of revulsion cramped her stomach, she thrust the door open and almost fell out of the car.

The sound of the sea drummed in her ears,

rolling out its sonorous invitation. She walked towards it, kicking off her shoes as sand dragged at her feet. Frothy crests glinted in the moonlight, endlessly moving, spilling on to the beach, beckoning her closer before coyly retreating. Wet sand squelched between her toes. It felt good. Cool water washed around her feet, sucking at them persuasively.

Eve's hands moved instinctively, ridding her body of clothes. She trod them underfoot, a grimace of disgust on her face. Such clothes did not belong in this place. There was nothing corrupt here, no perversion of nature, no trace of a sick, twisted society. Her gaze swept slowly around the cove. The sea had been beating on these rocks and sand for thousands of years and would probably do so for many more thousands of years, unchanged by so-called civilisation.

Again water swirled around her feet, seductively inviting. She followed its drag, welcoming the cold sting of the next wave as it broke against her legs. Urged on by a blind need to rid herself of tonight's events, Eve struck out past the breakers to where the water rose and fell in soft swells. Here it was peaceful, soothing, and she floated with the tide, bobbing mindlessly like a piece of driftwood.

An alien sound filtered through her ears. Its message tapped persistently on her brain until reason insisted it was the sound of a voice, a human voice. She rolled her head sideways, not quite believing that it was so. The sight of a man ploughing into the surf towards her was nervejolting.

Eve thrust her legs down, frantic to avoid facing anyone. She kicked out jerkily and just as she began to swim, her leg-muscles cramped with paralysing pain. Her mouth opened to emit a scream of agony. Water gushed in, choking the sound in her throat. Her legs were useless. She was sinking. Her arms flapped in panic. She broke surface for a moment but not long enough to gulp in air. Pain crippled her and the water was all around, endless pain and water. Her lungs were bursting with the need to breathe. She had to breathe.

Consciousness came with more pain. Her chest heaved convulsively as she coughed out sea-water. Eve whimpered in agonised protest as nausea compounded the torture in her legs.

'Stupid bitch! If you want to drown yourself, go do it on someone else's beach!'

The harsh invective was lost on Eve. She struggled to reach her legs. 'Oh God!' she sobbed, clutching at the knots of pain.

Other hands swept her feeble grasp aside. Eve collapsed back on to the sand while strong fingers massaged the cramped muscles. Slowly the tension eased until only a bearable ache remained. Eve unclenched her teeth and opened her eyes. The man was kneeling beside her, a huge, dark blur.

'Thank you,' she whispered.

He slapped the loosened muscles once more and stood up, a towering figure of a man, completely naked. Only then did Eve remember her own nakedness. She shivered as his gaze raked her from head to foot.

'The mermaid act is over for tonight. Get on your feet,' he ordered peremptorily.

Before she could gather strength enough to make a move he had leaned over and pulled her up. Eve's legs wobbled and she would have fallen if he had not caught her in time.

'Goddammit!' he muttered. 'I suppose I'll have to carry you.'

There was no gentleness in the arms which cradled her. Eve's breasts were crushed against a hair-roughened chest and the sand clinging to her body rubbed its gritty discomfort into her flesh. The enforced contact between her nude body and his brought a flood of embarrassment to add to her discomfort.

'Please. I can walk if . . .'

'Shut up!'

The sharp impatience of the man made her squirm. He held her more tightly.

'Please . . .' she began again.

'I'm not spending the whole bloody night on a cold beach pandering to you.'

'If you just let me go you won't have to worry about me.'

He ignored her, striding purposefully towards the road but not towards Eve's car, which was now some hundred metres behind them. Discomfort and embarrassment quickened into fear.

'Where are you taking me?' she squeaked, panic catching at her voice.

He reached firm ground and abruptly stood her on her feet. His hands gripped her waist, holding her steady while he drew in a deep breath and expelled it. Then he spoke, biting each word out with sharp emphasis.

'Look, lady! I'm not interested in you. Neurotic women are a bore. To put it plainly, you're just a headache. I'm tired. Because of you, I'm also wet and cold. I'm going back to my cabin to have a hot shower, get warm, and if it's at all possible, get some sleep. And you're coming with me.'

'I've got my car. You don't have to——'

'No way!' he snapped impatiently. 'If you think I'm giving you another chance to drown your woes, you can think again. I can do without a body washed up on the beach, not to mention the hassle of calling the police.'

'But I didn't mean to——'

'You're wasting your breath.'

'No, truly. I——'

'Oh, for God's sake! I saw the headlights come down the track and I watched to see what you were up to. You went straight for the sea and you weren't figuring on putting those clothes back on again. You churned right on in without a backward glance. A dead-set suicide if ever I saw one. You ignored my shouts and when you saw me coming you sank out of sight.'

'I got cramp and . . .'

'So it was cold. I'm cold. And I'm not going to stand here arguing. What you do with yourself tomorrow or next week is out of my hands, but tonight you came to my beach and made yourself my business, so just shut up and walk since you don't like being carried. My cabin is just behind that grove of trees.'

He had swung her around and pushed her in the right direction. Eve stumbled along. The hand on the pit of her back did not allow any choice in the matter. She did not have the strength to fight him, and besides, she was now shivering with cold. A small building loomed out of the darkness ahead. Obviously this had been the source of the flicker of light she had seen earlier. It was a log cabin, small and primitive. The front door was open. She hesitated on the step, panic attacking her once more at the thought of being shut in, alone with a hostile stranger and both of them naked. The man swept her inside and closed the door.

'Stand still while I light the lamp,' he ordered curtly.

Eve stood rooted to the spot, her mind too numb to direct any other action. It was an old-fashioned kerosene lamp. The man's face sprang to life in its yellow glow. It was a hard, imperative face, framed with thick, shaggy black hair. Straight eyebrows beetled over deeply set brown eyes. His nose was slightly hooked. The jawline was strong and square. Deep lines ran from cheeks to mouth, an attractive mouth which gradually thinned in irritation as he looked at her.

'I'll get the water-heater going. Grab a blanket off the bed and put it around you.'

Her eyes skittered away from his very masculine nakedness. The powerful physique was intimidating. A double bed stood in one corner of the room. A mohair rug lay across the foot of it. The man moved to a back door and disappeared outside. Released from his presence Eve snatched up the rug and wrapped it around her. She sat down on the bed. Her legs were trembling too much for her to do anything else and she needed to rest and recover some balance.

Haphazard thoughts darted in and out of her brain. She was too exhausted for any coherent thinking. It was much, much easier to simply sit still and wait for the man to tell her what to do. He had saved her from drowning. But for him she would be dead. Right now she was not sure if she was glad to be alive or not and she could not find the will to care about the immediate future.

'Come on. Water's running warm.'

She glanced numbly at the man, not heeding his words. The towel around his hips was reassuring. And he was older than she had first thought. His features had a settled maturity. Closer to forty than thirty, she mused, yet his body was that of a young man.

'Move, dammit! I've done enough carrying for one night.'

Eve forced her legs to obey. He beckoned her outside and she followed him along a short verandah to a room which was also lit by a lamp. It seemed to encompass several purposes. Fishing gear was stacked along one wall, laundry-tubs and work-table against another, and a makeshift shower at the end. Water was spraying down. The man felt its temperature before whipping off her rug and pushing her under it. He handed her a washer.

'Hurry up! I haven't got water to waste.'

Her slow movements annoyed him. With another exasperated mutter he slung his towel aside, stepped into the shower with her and reclaimed the washer. There was nothing gentle about the brisk way he set about wiping her free of sand. Her neck, back and legs were given a quick rub-down. Then he roughly swung her around to face him.

'Why, in God's name, would a woman with a body like yours want to risk drowning?' he demanded curtly.

The washer encircled her breasts and moved down, over her stomach, between her thighs.

'Wasn't thinking of drowning,' she mumbled as a treacherous warmth tingled through her body.

She grew more and more aware of the hand behind the washer and the masculine strength of the body so close to hers. Here was a real man. Not like Simon. This man was well and truly aware of her as a woman. She stared in fascination at the undoubted evidence of his male arousal.

With his self-appointed task completed, the man straightened and the powerful thrust of his loins was even more awesome. Her fixed gaze elicited a further sigh of exasperation.

'What the hell! I don't take a shower with a woman every day and you're not exactly ugly.'

His explanation fell on deaf ears. A wild mêlée of emotions was churning inside Eve. The shattering disillusion of finding the man she loved in bed with another man forced every instinct to cry out that she was a woman who wanted to be loved as a woman. Loved, desired, taken as a woman. To know, to feel how it would be, how it might have been if Simon had been the man she thought. If he had wanted her, been excited by her, like this man. She had been looking forward to her marriage night, the marriage night that would never come now. Frustration and thwarted curiosity and a thousand crying needs forced her hand out. She touched him, her fingers soft, tentative, wondering.

His swift intake of breath was followed by an instant rejection. He knocked her hand away, stepped out of the shower and hastily knotted the towel around his waist. He turned back to her with a glare of contempt.

'What are you? Some kind of nymphomaniac? Or do you simply get a kick out of living dangerously? The package might be tempting, but I'm not so starved for sex that I'll take anything that offers.' He turned off the taps and threw her a towel. 'Dry yourself and cover up. I'll make us some coffee. It might bring you to your senses.'

Eve knew she should be ashamed, knew that she should be shocked at herself, but the dull, empty feeling was back again. Somewhere in the back of her mind she was shocked but it did not seem to matter. It did not matter what this man thought of her either. He was a stranger, not of her world, here tonight and gone tomorrow. It was quite ironic, really. Far from being a nymphomaniac, she was a virgin whose virginity had never been even threatened.

She knew now why Simon had never wanted to make love to her, why he had insisted that her wardrobe consist of boyish clothes, why he had liked her hair kept short. He had explained his reluctance to consummate their love by claiming that he wanted a true bride. She had been flattered by his old-fashioned romanticism, pleased and proud that he valued her so much.

Eve sourly wondered what excuse he would have given on their wedding night, whether he would have been able to sublimate his true sexual inclinations and keep fooling her. It was lucky that she had found out before she was legally tied to him. But she did not feel lucky. She felt badly used. And yet she was not used. Here she was, all untouched, and likely to remain so. A bitter irony curved her mouth into a grimace. She was certainly safe from being touched by the man inside the cabin. She wrapped the mohair rug around her once again and returned to the main room.

The man had pulled on a pair of jeans and a sweater. He was standing at a gas stove, waiting for a kettle to boil. Two mugs were sitting on a roughly hewn wooden table. Eve pulled out a chair and sat down. Neither of them spoke. Clearly he did not like the situation and Eve had nothing to say to him. She was not about to explain her behaviour. He had taken control and brought her here. If he did not like it he had only himself to blame. The kettle whistled. He poured steaming water into the mugs and pushed one towards her.

'There's sugar there. No milk,' he stated flatly.

'I don't take either,' she muttered.

Models could not afford excess weight. Simon had drummed that into her. He had approved of her slim hips and long legs but had always been critical of her full breasts, even demanding that she wear a bandeau to flatten them for some photographs. 'Top models are not cows,' he had said disparagingly. A whole parade of his words and actions marched through her mind, stamping out a new dimension of meaning. She had been a blind, naïve fool not to have guessed something was wrong in their relationship. Simon had never been a manly man, not like the brooding figure across from her. His chair creaked. She glanced up to find him studying her with cold objectivity.

'I seem to know your face. Should I?'

Alarm screeched through her brain. The last thing . . . the very last thing she could afford was to be recognised. Her break-up with Simon would cause comment enough. A rumoured suicide attempt would hit the headlines. She forced her voice to be dull and careless.

'I don't see how. We've certainly never met before.'

He could have seen her face on magazine-covers whenever he passed a newsagency, on television advertisements, hoarding boards. But not quite the face he was seeing tonight, not a face washed clean of its artful make-up. He stared at her for a moment longer then gave a dismissive shrug. His glance fell to her hands.

'Not married?'

She shook her head, relieved that the danger was over.

'Man trouble?'

Her mouth twisted with disgust. 'You could say that.'

'It figures.'

The dry comment brought a painful flush to her cheeks. He was obviously applying her answer to a lot more than she had meant. That mad impulse to touch him must have seemed blatantly wanton.

'I'm sorry that . . . that I've disrupted your night and been so much trouble to you. I . . . I didn't think there was anyone here.'

'Lucky for you I was here. And still awake.'

'Yes. Lucky,' she echoed dully.

He sighed and stretched back in his chair, making it tilt backwards. 'Didn't he want you?'

Her gaze flickered up and for a moment the whole depth of her disillusionment was there in her eyes before she tiredly hooded them. 'No, he didn't want me. He wanted the image. Not me.'

There was puzzlement in his voice when he spoke. 'What image? You mean the face and the figure? Or are you someone . . .'

'No, no,' she said quickly, not wanting him to probe out her identity. The sick débâcle of her love for Simon billowed through her mind and all the bottled-up horror of the night burst out of her in tortured words.

'He doesn't want a woman. Not a real woman. We were going to be married. Next week. And tonight . . . he wasn't expecting me at his apartment. I went . . . the music was so loud he didn't hear me ring. I used my key. There was a smell—heavy, sweet—incense, pot, I don't know. It worried me. I went into his bedroom. He was with . . . with another man . . . and they were . . . they were . . . I . . . I ran out and just kept driving until I found this place.'

The tears which Eve had kept choking back for hours began trickling down her cheeks. The large green eyes were pools of misery, blind to everything but her inner grief. She did not see the flash of recognition on his face, nor the comprehension which brought a soft compassion to his eyes. Having found release, the tears continued to well up and overflow. Eve slumped forward, propping her head with one covering hand as she wept uncontrollably. Her heart seemed to swell to breaking point. Great racking sobs eased the constriction in her chest, and it was a long time before the sobs deteriorated into shuddering little sighs. She dabbed the wetness from her eyes with the back of her hand.

Only then did she become aware of fingers drumming a restless tattoo on the table. Her chest heaved once more as she struggled to pull herself under control. A furtive glance at the man caught the dark frown which pulled his eyebrows together into a heavy line. The fingers stopped tapping and she felt his gaze on her. Having bared her soul as well as her body, Eve felt even more naked. Her hand clutched the rug more closely around her, subsconsciously grasping for a protective cloak.

'Want to lie down?'

The quiet question brought a self-conscious flush to her cheeks. She hung her head, not knowing what to answer. All along the man had judged her harshly and she could not tell if he was being kind or critical.

'You must feel completely wrung out. It's been a very rough night on you, and I haven't

made it any easier.' He sighed and his hand
spread open in a gesture of appeasement. 'I'm
sorry for having been so . . . so unsympathetic.'

She darted a glance at him. He seemed sincere.
She swallowed nervously and forced herself to
speak.

'I really didn't think of drowning. It was just
. . . I felt . . . I needed . . .'

He waved a dismissive hand. 'You don't have
to explain.' Then in a softer voice, 'You're well
rid of him, you know.'

'I know,' she whispered, but her eyes were
haunted with the pain of emotional surgery.

He pushed himself to his feet, rounded the
table and gently squeezed her shoulder. 'Come
on. Into bed. You'll feel better in the morning.'

Taking it for granted that she would follow his
suggestion, he leaned forward and turned off the
lamp. Eve was slow to react. An arm slid around
her shoulders, lifting her upright and supporting
her for the few steps to the bed. It was not until
he tried to relieve her of the mohair rug that Eve
felt driven to protest.

'Please . . .'

'A little late for modesty, don't you think?'
came the dry comment. 'You won't need it in
bed,' he added as he pulled back the bedclothes
for her.

Eve hesitated, then realising that the darkness
cloaked her anyway, she let the rug go and
quickly slid between the sheets. The soft comfort
of the pillow and mattress felt incredibly good.
She stretched her legs and sighed before
languidly moving into her usual sleeping position.

The slight rustle of clothes whispered in her ear. Her head whipped around, her eyes wide open in alarm. The dark silhouette near the bed was tossing a garment aside.

'What ... what are you doing?' Eve choked out. It was perfectly obvious what he was doing but she did not want to accept it.

'Coming to bed.'

'With me?' she squeaked.

'There's only one bed. You surely don't object to sharing it with me,' he said reasonably.

'But ...'

'Look! I was wrong earlier and I made you feel bad. I didn't understand what you were feeling, the rotten kind of sexual shock you'd been through. No woman deserves to be hurt like that.'

He climbed into bed and before Eve could shrink away, his hand reached over and gently cupped her cheek. He propped his head up with his other hand and looked down at her.

'And you are very much a woman, a beautiful, desirable, totally feminine woman.'

She stared back, her mind exploding with the certainty that he meant to have sex with her. His hand trailed down her throat. She swallowed convulsively. It stroked across the line of her shoulder, featherlight in its touch. Her skin leapt with the prickles of tiny, electric shocks.

'Relax. I won't hurt you. Just unwind and let go. I'll give you the kind of loving you need.'

Eve's cry of protest turned into a strangled gasp. His hand had moved from her shoulder. It was closing over her breast, gently squeezing the soft fullness, his thumb brushing lightly across her nipple. Then his mouth was on hers and his body was moving, touching, pressing.

CHAPTER TWO

SHE had invited this. Nothing could have been more blatantly inviting than her action in the shower. So how could she stop him? What could she say? She had to say something. Eve opened her mouth. Any words she might have spoken were stolen from her tongue. The kiss which had begun as a tantalising touch on her lips, became a deep, sensuous exploration which took her breath away.

Her fingers blindly plucked at the hand which held her breast captive, but the sweet pleasure emanating from that hand weakened their purpose and they grew still. There was a strange exhilaration in feeling the hard length of his body against hers. Her skin was prickling with excitement and a treacherous hum of anticipation danced along her veins. Did she really want it to stop? Hadn't she wanted to know what it was like? All she had to do was let it happen.

A tiny voice of sanity screamed that it was wrong. She did not even know this man, let alone love him. It was wrong to let this intimacy go on. But her brain was being flooded by other messages, fascinating messages of unimagined pleasure, and slowly but surely they seduced that tiny voice of reason into complacency. A worm of guilt remained. With one of those odd side-steps the brain performs when a decision becomes too hard, Eve shut her eyes and pretended this was her wedding night.

He was not Simon, but Simon had cheated her. His love had been a deception. The sensations sweeping through her now were no deception. She had been holding back her response, but wanting now to feel the passion which had been denied her, Eve returned the kiss with fervour. Casting all inhibitions aside, she let her hands roam, finding that she liked the springy thickness of his hair, the muscular strength in the neck and shoulders above her, the firm flesh which was such a contrast to her own softness.

Her body arched its invitation, demanding his touch, wanting his exploration, begging to know the whole range of feeling that he promised. And he gave her what she needed with all the delicacy and finesse of a very experienced lover. Eve did not think of him as a person. He was touch, awakening her body to a life it had never known, fine-tuning it to a high pitch of pleasure, his mouth and hands finding and exploiting erotic zones she had read about but scarcely believed. She had been unable to imagine the incredible sensitivity which tingled with increasing pressure, demanding more and more satisfaction. There was an urgency which became a compulsion, so that her whole being was concentrated on one need, and the need had to be fulfilled. It was right, necessary, imperative.

Her body trembled in anticipation, every nerve-end aching for the entry which had been delayed for so long. She held her breath as it began. There was a hesitation, a withdrawal. Her breath rushed out in a sob of need. Her hands pleaded for it to be finished. There was a hard, driving thrust, a tearing pain, then body owning body in an act of possession which was totally dominant, throbbing with its own vibrant life, all-demanding until its demand was ultimately met, and Eve was floating on a different sea, her body bathed in a sweet, warm ecstasy she had never known existed. She sighed and the sigh was utter contentment, a beautiful measure of peace and satisfaction and total relaxation.

The man sighed also. He lifted himself away and Eve had a twinge of regret that it was over, that he was separating himself from her. There was a touch on her stomach, a light, sensitive touch which made her shiver.

'Are you all right?'

The deep voice held concern and Eve prickled with sudden embarrassment. She was lying here with a stranger, having just experienced the most intimate relationship with him. She wished he had not spoken. The words had broken into her self-absorption, forcing her to acknowledge him as a person. He stirred. She had to answer him.

'Yes. Yes, thank you.'

The words came out stilted, too formally polite for a situation which cried out for precisely the opposite. She choked down a bubble of hysteria as she faced up to the actual reality of what she had done.

'You could have stopped me at any time. I would have stopped. You had only to speak up.'

The edge of accusation in his tone struck her jarringly. Why was he blaming her? She had not seduced him. She would have kept rigidly to one side of the bed, left to herself. He had not seduced her either. Honesty demanded that she admit that truth.

'I didn't want you to stop.' Then understanding dawned. 'Don't worry. You won't be accused of rape.'

It was an ugly word, rape. It soured the pleasure he had given her. She rolled on to her side, turning away from him, but before she could settle comfortably he had pulled her back and was leaning over her again.

'Rape doesn't enter into it, as well we both know. But you should have told me you were a virgin. Goddammit! You didn't act like a virgin and it never occurred to me that you might be one.' He sighed and shook his head, and when he spoke again the anger had been replaced with a soft wryness. 'Well, I hope you enjoyed it because I can't roll the clock backwards. The devil of it is, I meant to help you, not create another problem.' He dropped back down on his pillow, moving his head restlessly until he put his hands behind it. 'And the truth of it is, I didn't want to stop either. I just hope you don't regret it.'

She had enjoyed it. Her body melted with the remembrance of pleasure as she recalled all the nuances of feeling. No, she did not regret the experience he had given her. She knew it all now. Knew how it felt to be a woman.

'I wanted to know,' she murmured, more in confirmation of her thoughts than in answer to his words.

Silence stretched between them, a more solid wall than any partition, yet their very separation forced a greater awareness of the man on to Eve. He lay very still and there was a quality of tension about him, of hard, concentrated thought. It suddenly struck her that Simon had been obliterated from her thoughts for a longer time than would have seemed possible a little while ago.

'Well, if it was what you wanted, why the hell should I care?' The words were muttered as if they underlined the final say in an argument. His breathing became more relaxed as if he was settling for sleep. Suddenly his head turned towards her. 'Why were you a virgin anyway? You're not so very young.'

'You know why.' She wished he would stop harping on the subject of her virginity. It recalled Simon too painfully.

'But surely there've been other men who wanted you,' he persisted.

'I loved him. No one else. Please don't go on. It doesn't matter.'

Eve thought how strange it was, lying here with a man she did not know, just voices in the darkness. The whole night had been strange, isolated from a life which used to make sense to her. Nothing seemed to make sense any more. Simon had turned into an alien and she herself had acted completely out of character.

'Tell me about yourself.'

She glanced sharply at the man, resentful of his intrusion into her reverie. He knew too much already, far too much to be admitted to her real life. She would die of embarrassment if she ever met him again away from here. What she had shared with him had been wonderful, a beautiful experience, and she did not want it spoilt. It was the one good thing that had happened to her this night. But it had to stop here.

'Do you live here all the time?' she asked, wanting the assurance that she was unlikely to run into him elsewhere.

'I come and go,' he answered vaguely. 'Where do you live?'

'In Sydney.' That was vague enough. It was a big city.

'What will you do tomorrow?'

'I don't know. I'll work it out as I go home,' she said despondently, hating the thought of explaining to her mother that the wedding was off.

'It's not going to be easy, is it? Better for you to stand back from it for a couple of days. You can stay here if you like.'

'I couldn't do that,' she said quickly. Her involvement with this man was too deep already.

'You need a breathing space. Time to get your head together. Ever gone fishing? It's a very restful occupation. Empties the mind of pressures.'

Memories from her childhood flashed into her mind and a wave of nostalgia softened her voice. 'I used to go fishing with my father. That was a long time ago.'

'Is your father at home?'

'No. He died when I was fourteen.'

'Do you live alone?'

'No. With my mother. She and I . . .' Eve clammed up, suddenly realising he was drawing her out.

'Do you good to stay a while . . . go fishing,' he said temptingly.

Suspicion wormed into her mind. 'Why should you invite me to stay? You didn't want me here before . . . before . . .'

'Before I found out that you weren't what you seemed to be? No . . . you're quite right. I would've shot you out of here as fast as possible.' He sighed and his voice took on a soft lilt of self-mockery. 'Maybe I want to make amends . . . maybe I feel a kind of responsibility . . . I don't know. I guess I'd like to make sure you're all right.'

'I'll be all right,' she muttered, rejecting his interest in her. That could only develop into complications she did not need. All the same, it was a tempting idea, to stay here, go fishing, postpone the moment of stress, the tears and argument which were inevitable . . . a temporary escape, not long, just long enough to build up some strength of purpose so she could cope. 'Do you think . . .' she hesitated, torn between caution and temptation.

'Do I think what?' he prompted.

'Could we . . . if I stayed here tomorrow . . . could we remain strangers? I mean . . . just being here . . . no questions asked,' she finished limply, hoping he would humour her but expecting him to laugh at her unease.

His silence made her feel like a silly child.

'Oh, forget it! I'll go,' she said decisively.

'No. I want you to stay. And you want to leave
it all behind you for a while. I'll play along with
that. After all, I come here for the same reason,'
he said slowly.

'That's . . . that's kind of you.'

He gave a short laugh, a slightly derisive
sound. 'Perhaps it's easy to be kind to a stranger,'
he mused. 'Are you feeling cold over there?'

'Not really.'

'I thought you shivered just then.'

'I'm not used to sleeping in the nude.'

He rolled on to his side and scooped her back
against him, curving her body to his. One hand
cupped a breast familiarly as his mouth grazed
over her ear. 'Relax now and go to sleep. I'll keep
you warm.'

Warmth flooded through her but she was far
too aware of his masculinity to relax and go to
sleep. He did. She heard his breathing grow
lighter and his hand slackened its hold. She lay
snuggled against him, marvelling at the comfort
another body could give. Eventually sheer
weariness took its toll and she drifted into sleep.

She woke suddenly, aware of a tingling caress
on her cheek. Her eyes widened in shock at the
strange face above her. It spoke and memory
surged back in a hot flood of embarrassment.

'Perfect skin. You really are a very beautiful
woman, even in the morning. I doubt that I've
ever seen such true blonde hair, except on a
child . . .'

Child! Had he recognised her? Her fingers flew
in agitation to her hair. Last night it had been
wet, uncombed. It was a relief to feel the loose

curls. Without the careful blow-waving which smoothed a frame for her face, she was not instantly recognisable as Eve Childe.

'Classic cheekbones, perfect features, and those sea-green eyes. Enough to steal a man's soul. Maybe I did catch a mermaid last night.'

The possessive note in his voice brought a sharp awareness of her vulnerability. Fear jabbed at her mind. She had been crazy last night, completely reckless to have put herself in the power of a stranger. So very intimately. She knew nothing of him. Nothing at all. Except that he was a good lover. Fear cut deeper. Did he now expect a repeat performance? She clutched at the bed-clothes, pulling them up around her chin. Her eyes darted around the room even while common sense told her there was no immediate escape from him.

'What ... what time is it?' she asked, swallowing hard to combat a very dry throat.

'Almost lunch-time.' Amusement gleamed in his eyes. 'And I'm not the big, bad wolf come to gobble you up. In fact, you could call me quite house-trained. I even found your clothes on the beach and washed them for you.' He nodded towards the end of the bed. 'Look for yourself.'

The silk culottes she had discarded last night were neatly folded.

'Not very practical for going fishing,' he added drily.

Going fishing! Eve choked back a hysterical little laugh. She really had been out of her mind to even contemplate such irresponsible behaviour. 'Thank you, but I really must go,' she said quickly. 'My mother will be worrying where I am.'

'I doubt it.'

Eve's breath caught in her throat as wariness jangled into alarm. What did he mean? Her eyes flickered nervously over the strong physique. His jeans and Tee-shirt emphasised the broad chest and muscular limbs. This was a lonely, out-of-the-way place and if he wanted to keep her here . . .

'My mother will be worried. If I'm not home this morning she might call the police.'

He shrugged and stood up, eyeing her with lazy mockery. 'Why should she worry? Weren't you with your fiancé last night? She'll draw the natural conclusion and not be overly concerned. After all, you're getting married next week.'

'I'm not . . .' Eve began in a fluster.

'We know that, but she doesn't. Why be in a hurry to tell her? Indulge yourself. You had a shock last night and it won't hurt anyone if you take a day off. Besides, you need the time to take stock of where you're going from here,' he said matter-of-factly. 'I'll go clean the fish for lunch. There's an outhouse beyond the laundry. Get dressed and take a stroll. No rush.'

She watched him cross the room to the door on to the verandah. His calm, unhurried air did much to soothe her nerves. He did not seem to pose any threat to her. She remembered their conversation last night after . . . her hand slid across her stomach and her thighs quivered as physical memories tingled around her veins. A warm glow suffused her body. Crazy it might have been, but she did not regret last night's madness. Not yet, anyway.

It took a concentrated effort to shrug off the
languor which tempted her to lie there. She
forced herself out of bed. Her eyes skated around
the room. It was certainly spartan in its
furnishings. The floor was cobble-stoned and the
only real concession to civilisation was the gas-
stove and the insect-screens on the windows. Her
gaze dropped to the silk culottes at the end of the
bed. She eyed them with distaste. Simon had
chosen them, insisting that they showed off her
cute behind. Grimacing at the thoughts which
that conjured up, Eve snatched them up and
pulled them on. They were hopelessly creased.
She wished there was something else she could
wear. With a sigh of irritation she did up the zip
and fastened the halter collar at the back of her
neck.

Now was the time to leave. The man was out of
the way. The sensible thing to do was walk out
the front door, return to her car and drive back to
Sydney. To stay was to risk ... She opened the
front-door and a light sea-breeze wafted over her
skin. Her eyes drank in the glittering blue of
sunlight on water, white, white sand, a cloudless
sky, marked only by swooping seagulls. She
breathed deeply, savouring the salty smell. It was
the smell of freedom from all the shackles of
society. What would she risk by staying here?
Just for a day. One lost day could not hurt.

The man did not know her. He seemed
friendly and reasonable. In all honesty she could
not say that he had pressed himself upon her last
night and his concern over her virginity suggested
a man of sensitivity. Surely such a person could

not represent any danger. And she would enjoy going fishing.

Her gaze followed the dirt track back to her car, still parked on the beach verge. Last night she had not even considered that the road might lead to a house, but last night her mind had been too distracted for clear thinking. Even now it shrank from the prospect of dealing with explanations and argument. She did not want to face up to the repercussions of the inevitable split with Simon. Not yet. Not when she could stay here for a while.

She walked outside and surveyed the house with curiosity. The log cabin fitted so snugly into the grove of trees that it looked to be part of the landscape. At one side were two large water tanks, partially camouflaged by native shrubs. She strolled around the back and spotted the small outhouse. It provided a decidedly primitive sanitary arrangement. Eve mused that civilisation did have its advantages, particularly in the plumbing department.

She hesitated over her return to the house, the impulse to stay becoming undermined by the necessity of confronting the man again. It was difficult to ignore the fact that she had slept with him. Her empty stomach growled its demand for food and the smell of cooking fish added its persuasion. The door leading on to the back verandah stood open. She approached it with caution, treading lightly so as to make no sound. There was still time to change her mind and go.

The man was standing at the gas-stove, watching a sizzling pan of fish. Again Eve was

struck by his strong masculinity. He had none of
Simon's litheness, the quick grace of movement
which she had thought of as refined elegance.
Even in casual clothes Simon had had style, not
that he would ever have worn old workman-like
jeans. The man across the room looked at home
in them. It occurred to Eve that he would look at
home in anything because it was not the clothes
which drew the eye, but the man himself. He
carried an air of self-assurance which suggested
he could handle anything that came his way. He
was the sort of man one would choose to have as a
companion on a deserted island.

A smile twitched at Eve's lips. For all intents
and purposes this was a deserted island, and he
was obviously cooking fish he had caught. His
head suddenly turned. Dark, piercing eyes
scanned her quickly and caught the trace of a
smile on her lips. The hard face relaxed. His
smile was rich with satisfaction. Eve's heart
thumped a warning but the reckless mood of last
night had taken hold again.

'Smells great.'

His smile widened into a grin. 'Nothing like
fresh fish.'

'I'll just wash my hands,' she said, nodding
towards the all-purpose laundry.

'Don't be long. These are ready to eat.'

'I'll be right back.'

It was not until water was splashing over her
hands that Eve realised her own facial muscles
were stretched into a grin. It surprised her. Yet
on second thoughts, it was not surprising. She
had thrown her cap over the windmill with a

vengeance and the resulting light-headedness was having its effect. Today she was going to enjoy herself and the rest of the world could revolve without her. It would catch her up eventually. That was unavoidable. But not today. A printed sign flashed into her mind. GONE FISHING. She laughed as she dried her hands. She was ready for breakfast, lunch . . . anything.

CHAPTER THREE

THE fish was delicious; tender, full of flavour, cooked to perfection. Eve ate with relish and poked at the bones for the last shreds.

'Want some more?'

She looked up at the man sitting opposite her. His eyes were crinkled in amusement. They were attractive eyes, dark, intelligent and very expressive.

'No. I'm just being greedy.' She put down her knife and fork and sighed with satisfaction. 'I can't remember the last time I ate so much for breakfast.'

'You had a very empty stomach.'

The wooden chair creaked as she leant back against it. It did not alarm her. The chair was strong and solid, like the rough-hewn table and the rough-hewn man. She observed him curiously as he lit a cigarette.

'Do you smoke much?'

He threw her a careless look. 'Do you object?'

She shrugged. 'I'm hardly in a position to object. It's your home.'

He exhaled the smoke slowly. Then his mouth curved into a dry little smile. 'So it is. I enjoy a cigarette after meals but no, I don't smoke much. Do you?' He nodded an invitation to the packet.

She shook her head.

'What would you like to do this afternoon?'

The question surprised her. 'Aren't we going fishing?'

'Tide's wrong. We'll try later on.'

His matter-of-fact tone dispelled the prickle of unease. Her gaze was drawn to the window, to the age-old appeal of sand and sea. 'I'd like to walk along the beach. Are there any shells?'

'Some.'

'I used to collect shells. I had a whole shelf of them.'

'Don't you still have them?'

She turned back to him with a wistful smile. 'No. When my father died we sold up and moved into the city. Mum insisted it was time I left childish things behind. And the apartment was too small for a lot of clutter. I missed them though. I always liked the sound of the sea and I could hear it in the shells.'

'Then maybe you should start another collection.' He stood and picked up their plates. 'I'll go wash these and we'll be on our way.'

Eve rose quickly to her feet. 'I'll do them. You cooked. Just tell me where to put the bones.'

He did not relinquish the plates but stood there looking her up and down in a slow, measuring way. Eve blushed, all too conscious of how well he knew her body.

'I could lend you a Tee-shirt if you want to save those clothes for later.'

'Thank you.' It was an embarrassed whisper and she forced more volume into her voice. 'You're very kind.'

His lips quirked sardonically. 'It'll hardly be

high fashion but a belt might help. You'll find
them in the chest of drawers near the bed.'

His crack about high fashion made her look
sharply after him as he strode out on to the
verandah. The suspicion that he knew her
identity crawled uncomfortably around her mind.
Uncertainty made her nervous and she stood
there, her fingers absently pleating the silk of her
culottes. The texture of the material gradually
impressed itself on her mind and she remembered
that he had washed them. He would have seen
the designer label. Surely that had prompted his
remark. Relief washed through her. She hurried
to the chest of drawers, found a Tee-shirt and
quickly discarded high fashion for casual slop-
piness.

Laughter gurgled up in her throat as she took
stock of her appearance. The sleeves began just
above her elbows and flapped above her wrists.
The crew-neck hung loosely around her shoulders
and the hem drooped unevenly around her
thighs. The soft cotton clung to her breasts but
barely touched her anywhere else. She found a
belt and gathered in a waist, making a most
inelegant mini-dress.

'Ready?'

He was leaning against the door-jamb, amusement written all over his face. Eve knew she
looked ridiculous but she did not care. Today it
did not matter how she looked. Today Eve
Childe did not exist. In her place was a carefree
woman. Carefree for a little while, anyway. She
almost skipped over to the front door and flung it
open in her eagerness.

'Let's go,' she called to him, a lilt of childish excitement in her voice.

They walked along the beach. Seagulls swooped overhead, the only other living creatures in sight. The breeze plastered the Tee-shirt around Eve's body and made it skirl around her thighs as she ran ahead of her companion. She was completely unaware of the sexiness of her makeshift dress. Her eyes were fixed on a large, spotted shell at the water's edge.

'It's a good one!' she shouted triumphantly, holding it aloft like a trophy. Then with a happy smile of anticipation she pressed it to her ear. The echo of the sea was distinct. Her face lit with pleasure as the familiar drone reverberated through her brain. Satisfied, she brushed the sand from her newly found treasure and polished it on her Tee-shirt.

'See! Isn't it beautiful?' she crowed in delight.

'Yes. Very beautiful.'

The deep appreciation in his voice carried overtones which jolted Eve out of her reverie. She glanced up into eyes which were not fastened on the shell in her hand. For a long moment their gaze locked and Eve's pulse beat louder than the drum-roll of the sea. He did not touch her, yet she could feel his touch. Her skin crawled with sensitivity and an aching weakness invaded her thighs. Her chest felt constricted and only when it became painful did she realise she was holding her breath. She expelled it quickly and forced herself to turn away from him, taking a few jerky steps before darting a glance back at him.

'Please don't,' she begged.

'Don't what?'

He had not moved but the dark eyes threw out a challenge which had to be answered.

'Last night ...' She took a deep breath to steady her voice. 'Last night—I don't regret it but it would be wrong to repeat it.'

'Why?'

Even his stance was a challenge. He was not threatening her but he was so very much a man, and his eyes told her she was very much a woman, and they were here alone, together, and he knew she would respond to him.

'I don't love you,' Eve explained, a note of fear in her voice as she fought his strong attraction.

'That didn't worry you last night,' he reminded her with relentless logic.

Her hands fluttered helplessly. 'I don't ... I'm not ...'

'Not in the habit of making love with strangers?' he finished for her. 'No one knows that better than I. But it was good, wasn't it?'

The soft words were seductive. Eve's body shivered, a traitor to her will. 'Yes, it was good,' she admitted reluctantly, 'but you're a real person now and I don't love you.'

He frowned. 'A real person?'

'Don't you see?' she rushed in anxiously. 'It was like a fantasy, an answer to a need.'

For what seemed an eternity his eyes burned into hers, demanding that she recall the intense reality of their bodies joined in intimacy. At last he turned his gaze out to sea, releasing Eve from the tension of conflict.

'A fantasy!' he muttered and gave a derisive

little laugh. 'Funny! I've thought of myself as
many things but never a fantasy.' He sliced her a
wry smile. 'Comes with fishing a mermaid out of
the sea, I guess.'

The fire of desire was quenched. Eve smiled
her relief. 'I'm not a mermaid.'

'No.' His eyes gently mocked her. 'You're
more of a child.'

The word jarred. Her smile faltered until she
remembered the shell in her hand. She looked
down at it and sighed. 'Perhaps that's what I'd
like to be today. A child with no worries.'

'Then so be it.'

The warm indulgence in his voice lifted Eve's
heart. She threw him a grateful look and he
laughed a deep, throaty chuckle.

'Perhaps innocence is bliss. Shall we paddle
along? You can pass me any shells you want to keep.'

It was pleasant strolling along the edge of the
water. Eve stooped now and then to pick up a
promising shell. None was as perfect as the first
one she had found. The man had rolled up the
legs of his jeans and was following her in a lazy
fashion, not too close but close enough to be
companionable. Occasionally he drew her attention to something; a bird, a ship on the horizon, a
pair of porpoises beyond the line of breakers.

A light piece of driftwood floated in on a wave
and Eve picked it up. She drew hop-scotch
squares in the firm sand and tried to throw a
broken shell into the top corner. It slid across the
line. The man retrieved it, pushed her to one
side, took careful aim and landed it dead-centre.
She grinned at him.

'Don't tell me you played hopscotch as a kid.'

'When my elder sister dragged me into it. She was a dreadful bully.'

Eve laughed. 'I can't imagine you being bullied.'

He smiled a very self-assured smile. 'I did get the better of her eventually.'

'Strange how times change. You don't see kids playing hopscotch any more.'

'They're inside watching television. The whole world watches television. It's easier than living,' he remarked cynically.

'But you prefer living,' she murmured, understanding now why he had failed to recognise her. Any regular viewer would have known her face.

'I prefer to make my own pleasure, yes.'

And he was very good at making pleasure, Eve mused before stifling the thought. She liked his company. He was an easy man to be with but she did not want to think beyond that.

'Let's bask in the sun for a while.'

He did not wait for her agreement but stretched himself full length on the warm sand above the water-line. She sat down near him, drawing her knees up and hugging them. He put his hands behind his head and closed his eyes.

'What do you do for fun and relaxation?' he asked lazily.

'I don't have much free time. I like reading.'

'What?'

'Travel books mostly. You can pick them up and put them down without losing the thread of a story.'

'Done any travelling?'

'No. Not yet. I will though. Have you?'

'Mmh. Too much. Too many places. Too many people.'

She eyed him curiously but his lids remained shut and his face was relaxed, revealing nothing. 'Is that why you've settled here?'

He did not answer immediately and Eve turned her gaze back to the endless fascination of the sea.

'I like it here,' he said slowly. 'It's peaceful. Natural. Unspoiled.'

'Yes,' she agreed dreamily. 'It's like we were on an uninhabited island and civilisation is far, far away.'

He gave a soft chuckle. 'But you don't want us to play Adam and Eve.'

She threw a wary glance at him but the gleam in his half-opened eyes was sheer devilment.

'That might invite Satan into Eden,' she retorted lightly.

'Get thee behind me, Satan,' he intoned, then added curiously, 'Are you religious?'

'Not in any formal way, but I believe in the Christian code of behaviour.'

'Do unto others as you would have done to yourself?'

'Yes. It's wrong to hurt people. To be dishonest. Lying and cheating,' she added bitterly, the image of Simon rising sharply to mind.

'Forget him,' came the terse order. 'Tell me where you would most like to travel.'

They talked of other countries, other people, other ways of life. It was pleasant, impersonal talk, taking Eve's thoughts away from herself. The afternoon sun beat into their skin. Eventually the man beside her stirred and climbed to his feet.

'Think I'll go for a swim. Coming?'

He had stripped off his shirt before Eve found her voice. 'You know I haven't a costume.'

He laughed. 'Neither have I, but who's to see? There's only us.'

'I . . . I don't think so,' she mumbled, averting her gaze from the hands which were unzipping his jeans.

'You're not likely to get cramp again. The water won't be so cold in the heat of the day. Besides, I'm here to look after you.'

The jeans were pushed down and he stepped out of them. Her gaze was irresistibly drawn to travel up the strong, muscular legs and higher. She flushed as she met his questioning eyes.

'Does nudity bother you? It's much more pleasant to swim naked than with clothes on, you know. A child wouldn't hesitate,' he added persuasively.

She privately acknowledged the truth of his argument but she was frighteningly aware of the body which had taken hers in such total possession. 'I'm not a child,' she muttered.

'No, you're a woman. An adult woman who shouldn't be choked up with fears and inhibitions. Why don't you let yourself feel free? It won't hurt anyone.'

He turned and strode towards the water, leaving her to make her own choice. He ploughed through the first line of breakers to where the surf was deep enough for him to dive. Eve watched his dark head bob up and down and thought about what he had said. The conventions which shackled her seemed foolish and unnecessary here. The water looked inviting. The sun was hot. She wanted to swim naked and feel the wet coolness on her skin.

She pushed herself up, took off her clothes and ran into the surf, not giving herself time for second thoughts. She felt gloriously alive, her whole body tingling with sensuous pleasure as the cold water slapped and caressed her. She let herself sink under its surface, enjoying the total submersion. A hand grabbed her arm and yanked her up.

'I'm all right,' she spluttered in protest.

'Just making sure. Keep your head above the waves for my peace of mind. Okay?'

'Okay,' she gave in readily, not wanting him to hover around her protectively.

He did not crowd her but stayed within easy striking distance. Eve swam, floated, wallowed in the freedom which she found so delightful. Only when her fingers started crinkling did she move back towards the beach.

'Had enough?'

'Yes. I'm turning blue.'

Over-conscious of his watching eyes, Eve kept her back turned to him. Consequently she did not see the wave which bowled her off her feet and churned her around. Strong arms lifted her up and held her steady while she coughed out the water she had swallowed.

'You got well and truly dumped. Didn't you see it coming?'

'No. I wasn't looking,' she gasped out between coughs.

'Need the kiss of life again?' he teased.

She threw him a look of reproof and having looked at him she could not tear her eyes away. The sheer vitality of the man held her captive. He was so big, so strong, so dominatingly male. Beads of water shivered on the powerful chest as it breathed in and out. Her mesmerised gaze lifted slowly to the mouth which knew how to kiss. She saw his smile die and a long breath whistled out from the barely parted lips. The hands which had steadied her took a more possessive hold.

He stepped towards her, closing the small gap between them so that the tips of her breasts pressed lightly against his deeply tanned skin. The contact was like an electric shock. Eve jerked away. Her hands lifted and pushed against his chest to prevent a repetition, but his hands had also moved, sliding down from her shoulders, down the curve of her spine and closing over the roundness of her hips. He thrust her lower body against his and the potent force of his desire defeated any defence she might have managed.

Her body had a will of its own and it responded instinctively, exulting in the excitement of sexual arousal. Dazed by the strength of her own desire she looked up at the face above hers as if searching for an explanation, something which might justify this tumult of feeling inside her. She knew so little of the man and yet he could awaken her most primitive instincts so that they clamoured to be satisfied.

His eyes demanded that she yield to him. They blazed with the exultant light of the victor on the edge of victory. They conceded nothing and Eve felt what little will she had to resist drain away. She wanted him to take her and as if he perceived that mental surrender, his mouth came down and claimed hers.

Eve's hands slid up around his neck. Her fingers thrust into the wet thickness of his hair, blindly urging on the passion which was leaping through her veins. His mouth devoured hers in an invasion which had her senses reeling. A wave crashed against them, forcibly ending the kiss. Churning water sucked at her legs. She was lifted and held tightly against his chest as he took her beyond the breaking surf to the calm swell of deep water.

It lapped around her breasts as he kissed her again, and she clung to him as he swept her with him into a whirlpool of sensuality. Then he was lifting her higher, arching her back so that his mouth could trail down her throat to her breasts. He licked the salt water from her nipples and so distracting was the fierce wave of pleasure that she was barely aware of the hand parting her legs, pushing them to either side of him where they drifted, weightless, and the firm muscles of his stomach felt good against her softness.

Slowly, slowly he guided her down until she felt hard flesh probing upwards. She cried out as he entered her but the penetration was swift and his mouth was on hers again, his hands moulding her body to his, and the sheer eroticism of that movement inside her stilled any thought of protest.

Eve was unaware of the sea, the sky, the birds

which wheeled around them. Her whole being was concentrated on an inner world which suddenly exploded like a volcano of molten lava, and the blissful warmth of it pervaded her whole body, melting her bones with its exquisite pleasure. She wound her arms around the body which supported her. Its strength was hers. They were one being and there was a wonderful sense of peace in their union. For a long time they stayed together, wrapped in their shared warmth, moving only with the gentle roll of the waves.

'Stay with me.'

The husky whisper slid into her haze of contentment. Lips brushed against her ear, making it tingle with awareness.

'Forget the whole damned world. Let there only be us.'

He lifted her face to his and kissed her, a long, drugging kiss of sweet persuasion. Eve wanted it to go on and on, blotting out reality, but even as she responded to the spell he was casting, Eve knew it had to end.

She had stepped too far out of her normal existence as it was. This wild, abandoned loving was totally foreign to her cautious nature yet she could find no shadow of regret in her heart for anything that had happened. She had wanted to shed all responsibility, be a free spirit following impulse and instinct without reason, without care. But to stay with this man would be like trying to prolong a dream. It could not last forever. Sooner or later reality would intrude, the dream would crumble.

'I have to go back.'

It was a mournful whisper and his arms tightened around her, pressing his claim. 'Let it go,' he urged. 'This is more real than anything you'll find back there.'

She sighed and laid her head on his shoulder. The temptation was great. Yet she had her career and time was a model's worst enemy. She had to go back. Her gaze swept slowly around the cove and came to rest on the small log-cabin. It had been a resting-place. The man had salved her emotional wounds and shown her what it was to be a woman, but this was lotus-land. It was time to leave.

She reached up and kissed him, a soft kiss of gratitude, a kiss meaning goodbye. 'Thank you, but I can't stay. I have obligations, people to be seen, and my life to sort out. You've been very kind, and understanding. I appreciate, very much, all that you've shared with me. I'll never forget it.'

She was withdrawing from him and he knew it. The sense of finality in her words was unmistakable. For a moment she thought he was not going to accept her decision. His hands cupped her face and his eyes burnt into hers, demanding recognition of what they had just experienced together.

'You must go?' It was more a challenge than a question, denying that her departure was necessary. She had a choice.

Eve was sorely tempted but the very strength of his attraction struck panic in her heart. She had already succumbed to him twice. To stay was to throw aside her whole upbringing, all the threads which had been the fabric of her life. And where would it lead? What would become of her? It was a gamble she could not take, yet the thought of leaving was suddenly very painful.

'I have to,' she cried, and it was a plea against the sense of loss which sharpened even as she spoke.

The dark brilliance of his eyes clouded. He slowly released her from their intimate contact and a helpless kind of despair clutched at her as his withdrawal cemented her decision.

'I'm sorry.'

'Don't be sorry. You're free to go. You were always free to go,' he stated in a calm, expressionless voice.

'Yes I know. But I . . .'

His hand lifted and soft fingers brushed across her lips, silencing her. He shrugged off the hard, impassive mask which had shuttered his thoughts and a smile lightened his face.

'It was beautiful while it lasted. Don't be sorry. Do you want to go now?'

She nodded. He was making it easy for her, just as he had made the whole afternoon easy, letting her do as she liked. Having made the decision it was better that she go quickly, yet she could not force her legs to move. She was suddenly and poignantly aware of having destroyed something precious, something of great value which she might never find again.

He took her hand and pulled her with him, helping her through the roughness of the surf to shallow water. 'You won't mind if I don't come up to the cabin with you?' he said casually. 'I'll go along the beach and pick up my clothes.'

'I ... all right,' she agreed awkwardly and watched him stride away from her.

The separation was complete. Eve trudged up the sand, agonising over her decision with every step. She had come to this beach to escape, and she had. Only somehow the escape had gone too far, becoming an entity of itself which had irrevocably changed her life. Now as she walked to the cabin she felt dislocated, caught between two different worlds, belonging to neither. Yet the heavier weight of years and custom had demanded her return to what she knew.

The cabin seemed very empty without the man to dominate its space. It really was a comfortless place, bare and primitive, a stark contrast to the luxury of home. She hurried over to the bed. It took only a minute to don the silk culottes. Her gaze lingered briefly on the rumpled pillows, remembering how he had cradled her into sleep last night. Again she felt the wrench of parting. Tears pricked at her eyes and she moved blindly to the door, shutting the memory quickly behind her. She took a deep, steadying breath and set off down the track.

He was standing by the car, the Tee-shirts slung across one shoulder, the powerful chest still bare, his jeans clinging damply to the strong, muscular thighs. His eyes held a wry gleam as they looked her up and down, but he smiled as he lifted a hand towards her.

'Your shell. I thought you might like to keep it.'

She took it and a huge lump rose in her throat as she fingered its perfection. 'Thank you,' she choked out huskily.

'Eve, if you want to come back . . .'

The use of her name stilled her heart in mid-beat. Shock deafened her ears to what he was saying.

'You called me Eve!'

The strangled accusation brought no denial. He frowned in irritation but there was no puzzlement over her words.

'You know who I am!' she cried in hurt protest at his knowledge.

'So? What does it matter?' he said carelessly, as if the whole point was irrelevant.

But it did matter. She had not been a stranger to him, not just a girl who had happened along. He had known she was Eve Childe.

'When did you recognise me?'

He shrugged. 'Sometime last night while we were sitting at the table. You do have a well-publicised face, you know,' he added with a touch of irony.

Last night. Before he had made love to her. It was like a punch in the stomach. Her memory darted back over the sequence of events. He had been almost brutal to her after he had fished her from the sea, not one kind word or action. It wasn't until just before they went to bed that his manner had changed. She felt sick. All the loving and kindness had been for Eve Childe. She had wallowed in a fool's paradise while he had amused himself with her.

'Just what did you hope to gain by this?' she demanded bitterly, her eyes blazing with scorn.

'Gain?'

The surprise in his voice grated over the rawness of her humiliation.

'Oh, don't pretend you didn't expect to gain something! It's been a great game, hasn't it? Feeding me enough rope to hang myself?'

He frowned and his feigned puzzlement incensed her even further.

'You couldn't climb into bed fast enough, could you? Not when you realised who I was. It didn't matter a damn that I was too worn out emotionally to care what happened to me. That only made me an easier mark. Did it boost your ego to know you were making it with Eve Childe? Or were you already thinking of how you could work the situation to your advantage? No doubt you thought I'd be a good meal-ticket for you to latch on to. Or failing that, you could set up a red-hot story to sell.'

His face had tightened and hardened during her wild tirade. He waited for her to run out of breath then spoke with cutting coldness. 'Eve Childe holds no attraction for me whatsoever. The last thing I would want or need would be a woman to support me, and I can pay my own way without stooping to selling scurrilous stories.'

Eve was too worked up to heed the dangerous glint in his eyes. 'Huh! I suppose you live like this out of choice!' she scoffed. An ugly laugh of self-derision grated out of her throat. 'God! I must have looked like pennies from heaven to you! A lay-down gift just asking to be exploited. But let me tell you, you'll only make trouble for yourself if you take this story to a scandal rag. I'll deny it categorically and if you come after me I'll——'

He slapped her.

She stared at him, open-mouthed, her hand instinctively covering the sharp sting on her cheek.

'You blind, stupid fool!'

His biting anger frightened her more than the slap. She shrank back against the car, terrified that he meant more violence. His lip curled in derision at her fear and the dark eyes stabbed her with contempt. He waved a curt dismissal as if she was unworthy of his attention, then swung on his heel and began striding away.

'Go home, little girl!'

He had not bothered turning his head but the savage mockery in the words reached her nonetheless. Eve snapped out of her shocked daze. A turmoil of emotion churned into seething life.

'You . . . you bastard!' she screamed after him and hurled the shell in a frenzy of hurt and frustration.

Her aim was hopelessly astray. He kept on walking without so much as a hesitation in his gait. Recognising the futility of expending any more energy on a man who was ignoring her, Eve flounced into the driver's seat, revved up the engine with angry emphasis and spun the wheel for home.

CHAPTER FOUR

LITTLE girl indeed! She had been woman enough
for him last night. And this afternoon. He had
not hesitated to take full advantage of her pliancy.
Fool that she had been, letting a stranger make
love to her! She had recklessly disregarded all the
tenets of common sense. The fantasy of freedom
had beckoned and she had tested it to the full.
Crazy not to realise that the dregs were bound to
be bitter!

Damn the man! He had been amusing himself
with her. She remembered with smarting clarity
the 'high-fashion' remark, and his deliberate use
of the word, 'child'. She had been so easily
deceived, a gullible dupe, wanting to believe her
secret was safe. She should have guessed last
night when he suddenly stopped considering her
a neurotic bore and saw her as a desirable
conquest.

Eve Childe! He had made love to the image,
not the woman. The age-old allure of the boy-girl
image, that's what Simon had fashioned. It had
been a hit success; the slightly fey quality, the
teasing mixture of youthful innocence and
sexiness. Her long, coltish legs had always been
emphasised in shorts or slacks of one kind or
another, a provocative contrast to the soft
femininity of her face and the hint of vulnerability
in the green eyes. The image had sold well, at

very high fees, but the stranger had got it very cheaply. A gift.

No wonder he had been surprised at her virginity! No doubt he had thought that all models slept around. It was true that propositions were commonplace in her line of work. He was not to know that her mother and Simon had always protected her from men like him, men who took sex for granted.

Tears stung her eyes. She had given herself to him so ... so unreservedly. It had seemed right, unbelievably beautiful, an experience to be treasured. There had been something idyllic about two people coming together like that with no outside considerations influencing them, a pure attraction where names and backgrounds didn't matter. Eve gritted her teeth to prevent a sob emerging from the tightness in her throat. She would not cry over him. He had deceived her. For what purpose she did not know, could not even guess and did not want to. She had to forget him, put the whole incident behind her as if it had not happened. She had to get on with her real life, and to do that she had first to get home.

She forced herself to think ahead. Her mother would have to be placated and Eve could not tell her the truth of her prolonged absence. Then there was Simon. Pure hatred burned across her mind. No matter how much it might affect her career she was going to sever all connection with Simon. Pride and self-respect demanded that.

She concentrated on making plans for the future and gradually the long drive soothed her ragged nerves. It was almost dark when Eve finally garaged her car underneath the apartment building. Her tired gaze noted Simon's Volvo in the visitors' bay. She felt physically and emotionally exhausted and the thought of confronting Simon right now triggered a dangerous mood of angry rebellion.

She pushed herself out of the car, locked it, then strode towards the lifts, eyeing the Volvo balefully as she passed it by. She wondered how long it had been there and what Simon had told her mother. Certainly not the truth. The truth would be far too unpalatable for Marion Childe's digestion, despite her cast-iron constitution. A lot of things could be stomached along the road to success, but there was a limit to what one could swallow. Marion Childe had deliberately encouraged Simon's interest in Eve but even she would see that marriage was out of the question.

Eve summoned a lift and stepped inside, automatically pressing the button for her floor. It suddenly struck her that she had been thinking of Simon without pain, with disgust and contempt, but without even a twinge of the pain she had felt last night. She was surprisingly calm, almost as if the ugly scene in Simon's apartment had happened years and years ago, to someone else. The floor bumped to a standstill. The doors opened. Eve gave herself a mental shake and walked out. Her apartment key had barely touched the lock when the door was flung open.

'Eve!' Marion Childe gathered her daughter in. 'You're home, thank God! I've been at my wits' end worrying what to do.' The flood of anxiety was abruptly interrupted by a critical frown.

'And look at your lovely clothes! What on earth have you been doing all this time?'

Eve made no immediate reply. Simon was coming forward, a mute appeal in the vivid blue eyes. She found herself observing him in a curiously detached way. It was the same Simon she had fancied herself in love with; the same golden tan skin, streaked blond hair and blue, blue eyes; the same handsome face and lithe body, elegantly clothed as always, yet he had lost all his attraction. In fact she found his dress rather effete, too consciously perfect, as if too concerned with projecting an image. Of course! Simon dealt in images. Specialised in false images. Just as their oh-so-romantic love had been false.

'Eve.'

She recoiled from his outstretched hands. He smoothly waved them in a placating gesture.

'You shouldn't have rushed away like that,' he began softly, indulgently, as if she was a child who had acted without thinking.

Eve bridled at the tone even while recognising it as a tone which Simon and her mother had often used when she was being difficult. And she had all too frequently given in to it, accepting that they were older and wiser than she. Not any more would she give in to them. Eve gritted her teeth and turned to her mother.

'I'm sorry, Mum. I should have called and told you I was all right. It was selfish of me but I needed time alone to think.' Her voice sounded cool and calm, so self-assured that Eve was amazed at herself. Had the last twenty-four hours wrought so much change in her?

Marion Childe showed her surprise at the unexpected command in her daughter's manner. 'Well, so long as you're safe and sound. But your clothes, dear, you've ruined them. They'll never be the same——'

'Is that all you can think about, Mum? My clothes!' Eve flared, and all the bottled-up resentment of years came seething out. 'All my life it's been clothes, clothes, clothes! Don't play, Eve. You'll get your dress dirty. Sit up straight, Eve. Your skirt will crease if you slouch. What am I? A doll or your daughter? Did you ever consider that a person lived inside the clothes you dressed me in? Did you, Mum? Do you even care what I'm feeling now, or is a pair of silk culottes more important to you?'

'Eve!' The shock on her face was countered by the reprimand in her voice. 'Of course I'm concerned about you. It's just that your clothes cost so much. You know that!'

'Yes, I know,' Eve sighed, knowing full well that her outburst had been futile.

Appearances would always be of first importance to Marion Childe. However much anxiety she had suffered today, it had not stopped her from being immaculately dressed. The tailored pantsuit was not the least bit crumpled. Her long, ash-blonde hair was smoothly groomed into a French roll. An artful make-up hid the few wrinkles which aged the lovely face. For the first time in her life Eve felt sorry for her mother. Marion Childe would never know the heady delight of freedom from all social restraints.

'Well, I won't be wearing these culottes again,

Mum, so you'll have to write them off as a dead loss,' she added decisively, determined now to cast off the habit of following her mother's dictates. She was a person in her own right, and no longer a little girl to be told what to do. Certainly not a little girl!

She turned a cool face to Simon who had backed off from the line of fire. 'I wasn't expecting to find you here. Since you are, we might as well use the opportunity to settle everything right now.'

'Eve, now don't be too hasty,' her mother warned. 'Simon has been very distressed about last night's argument and I'm sure . . .'

'Argument, Simon?'

The green eyes mocked his evasion. An unbecoming flush spread up his neck, making him look surprisingly callow.

'Eve, I swear to you that if you'll let me explain . . .'

'No explanation is necessary. Our relationship is finished, Simon. Permanently.'

His expression hardened as his self-interest was threatened. 'You need me, Eve. Without me——'

'Like hell I need you!' she retorted scornfully.

'Eve! For goodness sake, will you listen to reason?' her mother demanded.

Eve turned on her. 'No! I won't listen to any damned reason for continuing with him.' She stalked away from them, impatient with the whole scene. The seeds of rebellion had been sown on a beach a long way from here but their growth was rapid in the cloying atmosphere in this room. She seated herself carelessly on one of the lounge-chairs in the living-room and faced them with an air of complete self-possession.

There was a short, fraught silence while her mother took stock of the defiant determination Eve had shown. She glanced worriedly at Simon then pasted a conciliatory smile on her mouth.

'Eve dear, you're obviously overwrought . . .'

'On the contrary, I am perfectly clear-headed. In fact, I doubt that I've ever seen things so clearly. If you'd like to sit down, Mum, I'll tell you what I have in mind.'

The smile shrivelled. Marion Childe sighed and fluttered an apologetic gesture at Simon. Eve resented the apology but made no comment.

'I'll make some coffee,' her mother said, clearly playing for time. 'Would you like something to eat, dear?'

'No thanks, and I don't want coffee. I'm tired and I'd much prefer Simon to leave. Right now.'

'Now look here, Eve——' Simon began as he stepped forward aggressively.

'I looked, Simon, and I finally saw a great deal,' Eve whipped back at him. 'I don't owe you a damned thing!'

'I made you.'

'Into what you wanted. Am I supposed to be grateful for that? So the image was successful. You made as much out of that as I did. As of now the partnership is dissolved. Come Monday I'll be giving my name to the top agents in town and I'll take my luck with them.'

'Eve, that's not fair,' her mother protested. 'Simon has——'

'Mum.' Eve's eyes flashed a warning. 'I'm

through with being pushed, your way or his. I'm twenty-two years old. I have a mind of my own and I intend to do what I want. I appreciate the fact that you've both worked hard at turning me into a success, but it wasn't so much for me as for yourselves. You wanted the success, much more than I did.'

Her mother looked at her as if her daughter had turned into a stranger. She shook her head and sank into the nearest chair. 'I don't understand what's happened to you, Eve. Why are you acting like this? I'm your mother and I've only ever done what's best for you.'

'I know you think that, Mum,' Eve said more softly, but the truth had to be said. 'The problem is that what you think is best for me is not what I think. It's time you stopped living through me. I have to live my own life. I'm not your little girl, Mum. I'm a woman.'

For one sharp moment her mind flashed to another place, sand and sea and a hard, demanding man who had known her as a woman. It took a concentrated effort to push the memory away.

'A woman!' Simon burst out angrily. 'You've no more sense than a baby! You're not seeing anything clearly at all. Your ego's had a knock and you're suffering from a swelled head, thinking you can launch out on your own. It's my photographs that've made you. Do you think any tin-pot photographer can capture the same effect?'

'We'll see, won't we?' Eve replied silkily, not rising to his taunt.

The handsome face twisted with disgust. 'God! If you weren't such a stupid innocent you'd see which side your bread was buttered on. Together we can go right to the top and I don't mean here. New York . . . London . . . Paris.'

'No!' The green eyes filled with contempt. 'I'm not so innocent, Simon, thanks to you. And it so happens I prefer margarine to the butter you're offering. Go find yourself another girl to mould into what you want. I'm not available, not even for the promise of New York, London or Paris.'

'You're cutting off your nose to spite your face,' he hurled at her in exasperation.

'It's my face,' she stated coldly.

Her stubbornness made him bare his teeth in frustration. 'You'll come crawling back to me when you find yourself a flop.'

'Don't count on it.'

'It's not good practice to burn your bridges before you cross them, Eve,' he said tightly. 'I can see there's no talking sense to you now. Try a little fling on your own. See how far you get without me.' He strode to the door, then turned to her with a sour smile. 'I'll even forgive your ingratitude when you finally admit you're wrong.'

Eve disdained to make any reply to his exit line. She could only feel relief at his departure.

'He's right, Eve,' Marion Childe said reproachfully. 'You just don't realise . . .'

'Don't I, Mum?' She turned soul-weary eyes to her mother. 'Then I'll have to find that out for myself.'

Her mother held out placating hands. 'Eve, let's talk about it.'

'No.' Eve knew that tone from old. It meant Mother knows best. She pushed herself to her feet. 'I've said it all, Mum, and I meant every word. I'm going to have a long bath. Later, if you want to talk about us, we'll talk. But not about Simon.'

As she lay soaking in a tub of warm water, memories of other water seeped into her mind and for a little while she gave them full flood. It was easy to rationalise the foolishness of her first surrender to the man's love-making. She had been off-balance, too emotionally disturbed to counter his physical persuasion. But she did not understand what had driven her into that second wild passion. Time, place, circumstances; she simply did not know.

It was fortunate that she had decided to leave before she had irrevocably placed herself in the man's power. He had deliberately deceived her and whatever motive he had nursed in keeping back his knowledge of her identity, one thing was certain. He could not have been trusted any more. Grimly Eve wondered if any man could be trusted.

She heaved herself out of the bath and slowly dried herself. Her body reacted sharply to touch and Eve wondered how long it would take to forget the physical magic it had been taught. At least there was no risk of her becoming pregnant from this mad escapade. Her preparation for marriage provided an inbuilt safeguard from her folly.

Her mouth thinned as she thought of Simon. Never would she crawl back to him, not in a million years. She put on a house-robe and walked out to the kitchen, hungry now, and ready to do battle with her mother if necessary. She wanted to be friends with her but she would not accept domination.

Marion Childe began by treating her daughter as an invalid, someone who needed to be cosseted and indulged. Eve was wryly amused by the tactic. She did not fight it. Only time would make her determination clear and eventually her mother would have to come to terms with an adult daughter. Marion Childe's ambitions had to be steered away from Eve and on to herself. She was a very good-looking woman and still young enough to do something constructive with her life. It had been blindly obsessive to channel all her energy into pushing Eve forward. Now that the first step of independence had been taken, there was no need for Eve to give more hurt by rushing too far too soon.

On Monday Eve cancelled all the wedding arrangements, then took portfolios of photographs to the top modelling agencies in Sydney. Their enthusiasm over adding her name to their lists was slightly dimmed by Eve's insistence that she would not work with Simon Trevaire. She remained adamant against reasoning even though she knew the arguments were valid. Her name had been linked with Simon's from the outset of her career. They had been a team, Eve Childe and Simon Trevaire. The agents were doubtful of selling her name without the photographer who had given it its individuality, and even more doubtful when Eve told them she did not particularly want to continue with the image Simon had created for her.

In the frustrating weeks which followed, Eve found that their doubts were justified. The offers came, but always with the proviso that Simon be behind the camera. She turned them down flat. She was warned that she was committing career suicide and Eve began to despair that she could make it on her own. She found no sympathy at home.

'Headstrong foolishness!' her mother ranted, having decided that Eve was not an invalid after all.

Marion Childe was equally headstrong, determined to steer her daughter back on to the course which she had set from the time Eve was a teenager. It was she who had sought out Simon Trevaire and virtually presented him with Eve, and while she now deplored his duplicity, she was still prepared to insist that Eve work with him. Eve ignored her mother's nagging but she felt very much alone as each fruitless day passed.

And rising in ever stronger waves from her subconscious, came the wish that she had not returned to this life at all. That one stolen day retained its spell despite how many times Eve reminded herself of its sour ending. The man could not be forgotten and her memory of their brief relationship always brought with it a deep, uncontrollable yearning. She had not felt alone with him. He had known her on a level which no one else had ever shared. If only it was possible to go back. But it wouldn't be the same—couldn't be—not after the way it had ended. Yet sometimes the call of sand and sea . . . and the man, was so strong it squeezed her heart unbearably.

There seemed no way to counter it. She told herself she was indulging in fantasy. Even if he had spoken the truth and there had been no crass ulterior motives in his action. Even if she crawled back and apologised and they could recapture their feeling for each other . . . and if all those ifs were fulfilled, there was still no real future with him.

He had not offered a future. Just—stay with me. And what had that meant? How long could one live an aimless existence, drifting around a beach, fishing, making love? Making love. She had to wrench her mind away from the seductive memories and transplant them with practicalities. One could not ignore the facts of life. Somewhere in her future she wanted marriage, children, and in the meantime she had to find work and make a living. Only there was no joy in the facts of life. Not like on the beach with the man.

There was certainly no joy from the modelling agencies either. Her career was fast becoming a non-event. When one of them finally called with a glimmer of hope she was ready to accept anything. It was not a firm offer. The Lamarr Corporation had only requested an interview with her but the request at least showed interest. An appointment was quickly arranged and Eve felt a prickle of excitement.

The Lamarr Corporation was the most prestigious cosmetics firm in Australia. As long as Eve could remember their products had been promoted by international stars, actresses and top-name models from the United States, Britain or Europe. If this interview meant they were considering Eve as the next Lamarr girl, it was the opportunity of a life-time. If they chose her there would be no lack of offers in the future. Her name would be well and truly made, not only here but on the international market.

Eve did not tell her mother about the appointment. If the interview was successful it would be soon enough to share the news. Then Marion Childe would have to eat all the negative words she had thrown at her daughter. Eve hid her excitement but her resolve to keep the interview a secret crumbled on the night before the appointment.

Simon Trevaire came to visit. It was immediately apparent to Eve that her mother had invited him. She faced them both with seething resentment as they hammered facts at her, demanding that she bend to reason.

'Be sensible, Eve. Publicity is everything in this game,' Simon insisted ruthlessly. 'Unless your face is seen continually you'll lose your buyer appeal. Put aside the personal element and work with me on a strictly business basis. You're losing more than I am, you know. My work's always in demand.'

'He's right, dear. You've been stubborn long enough,' her mother backed up predictably.

Eve retaliated with the only weapon in her armoury. 'Is that so? Well it might interest you to know that I have an interview with the Lamarr people tomorrow. And that, I might add, promises to do more for me than you ever did, Simon.'

'An interview is not a contract,' he scoffed.

Nevertheless his certainty in her need for him was shaken and Eve pressed her advantage. 'But you don't know that, do you, Simon? I'll take my chances with them, thanks very much.'

He sent her a malevolent look as he stood to go. 'I won't come again, Eve.'

'I didn't ask you to come at all,' she replied pointedly.

Marion Childe saw him to the door and they stood muttering their mutual exasperation for a minute or two. As soon as Simon had left her mother turned on Eve accusingly.

'Why didn't you tell me?'

'Why didn't you ask me if I wanted to see Simon?'

'Someone had to take a hand in getting you back together,' she explained curtly.

'I don't want your hand directing my affairs, Mum.'

'You're letting it all go down the drain with your stupid wilfulness.'

'I don't care if it does. I won't go back to Simon.'

But she did care. She desperately wanted a chance to prove she could make it on her own. After all, she was not trained for any other work and the future was beginning to look very uncertain.

The same sense of desperation dragged her feet

as she walked up the wide terrazzo steps to the Lamarr building the next morning. They had to like her. Her gaze lifted to the gold emblem on the large glass doors. If this prestigious firm decided to use her then the fear which had begun worming around her heart could be banished. Eve pushed one of the doors open and walked into the coolness of marble, a high vaulted ceiling and cascading water. The fountain was a statement of pure luxury and that was the hallmark of Lamarr products. They were luxury items, outrageously expensive but in a quality class of their own.

Eve glanced nervously at her watch. Still ten minutes before her appointment. She checked her appearance in the mirrored wall behind the fountain. The soft green of the silk suit emphasised the colour of her eyes and the hairdresser had done his usual professional job. The Eve Childe of her photographs looked back at her, perfectly constructed for this most important interview. She was not quibbling about her image this morning.

Satisfied that she could not have presented herself any better, Eve headed for the bank of elevators on the side wall and pressed the button for the Public Relations Floor. John Lindsey headed the department and he was the man she was to see. Eve took several deep breaths to steady her nerves as the compartment lifted and moved silently upwards. When the doors slid open she had fixed a smile on her face and for once she was pleased to see the gleam of envy in the receptionist's eyes. It boosted her confidence.

John Lindsey greeted her with more reserve
than she was accustomed to receiving from PR
men. He was tall and slender, well presented in
the young, executive style. He was not handsome
but not unattractive either. His smile held charm
and the quick, appraising eyes glinted with
appreciation. He was the kind of man who could
readily put both men and women at ease.

'Miss Childe, I've looked forward to meeting
you in person,' he said politely as he saw her
settled in a chair. He returned to his desk with a
brisk step then flashed her a disarming grin.
'Sometimes the camera lies but that is assuredly
not the case with you.'

'Thank you,' Eve murmured, grateful for the
compliment.

The grin disappeared. He assumed a business-
like air and launched into crisp speech. 'I'll come
straight to the point, Miss Childe. We've
developed a new perfume and we want the right
girl to sell it to the public. It has been our
standard policy to use big-name stars for
publicity campaigns, but . . .' He paused as if
choosing his next words cautiously. '. . . this
perfume is different, unique. We thought a
different approach might be more effective. Your
name was put forward as a possibility and we
would like to explore that possibility. I say
explore because our board of directors is not
convinced that you can present the right image.'

He threw her a little smile of encouragement as
if to reassure her that he thought she would be
right. The waggle of his eyebrows said it was out
of his control. Eve appreciated the byplay of

expression but it only increased her inner tension. He continued.

'What we'd like to do is make a pilot commercial with you. We'll pay you your normal fee but there's no guarantee that the commercial will be used. You may not care to waste your time without such a guarantee, but on the other hand, if you win approval with your work, the rewards will obviously be great. Apart from its financial aspect, a contract with Lamarr is quite a reckoning force in the fashion world, a fact I'm sure you appreciate.'

'Yes, I do,' she agreed quickly.

'Then perhaps you would like time to consider our proposition,' he invited magnanimously.

There was nothing to think about. Eve had no other choices in the offing. The opportunity to prove herself was dangling in front of her and she grasped it with eager hands. 'No. I'm quite happy to go along with that arrangement.'

'You understand it may lead nowhere,' he repeated insistently, almost apologetically. He really was very charming.

Eve smiled, unable to contain her excitement over the offer. 'On the other hand, it's a chance worth taking, isn't it?'

He smiled back. 'I thought you'd see it that way. Our Legal Department has an agreement drawn up for you to sign but Mr Lamarr would like to see you first. Excuse me a moment.' He leaned forward and pressed a button on his desk intercom. 'Please inform Mr Lamarr that I'm bringing Miss Childe up now.' He stood and there was no doubt that he was pleased with the situation. 'If you'll just accompany me?'

Eve rose gracefully to her feet. 'You said Mr Lamarr. I thought Margot Lamarr . . .'

'The queen has abdicated in favour of her son,' he explained with a touch of dry amusement. 'Margot Lamarr retains the title of Chairman of the Board and still fronts for the business, but it's Paul Lamarr who runs the company. It's not commonly known but make no mistake about it. He's the one you have to satisfy in order to seal a contract. And he's a hard man to please,' he added with a telling sigh.

Eve's nervousness returned as they rode an elevator up to the Executive Floor. Her stomach cramped into knots and she frantically tried to relax. It was clearly so important to impress this man. She had to be calm, self-assured, and above all, she had to convince Paul Lamarr that she was the right girl to sell his perfume.

She barely took in the sleek expensiveness of the reception area. John Lindsey nodded an acknowledgement to the woman at the desk. She waved towards a door and Eve was led straight to it. The PR man knocked before opening it but he ushered Eve inside without waiting for an answer.

It was a huge, streamlined office but Eve had eyes for nothing but the man who slowly rose to his feet. The grey suit was tailored perfection but he might as well have been dressed in jeans and Tee-shirt or nothing at all. It made no difference. He was the man from the beach, the man she had slept with in a primitive log-cabin, the man who had haunted her dreams ever since. And he was Paul Lamarr.

CHAPTER FIVE

HE stood there, tall, powerful, so clearly master of the situation, as the head of such a company would be expected to look. He acknowledged the formal introduction with a faint smile then addressed his PR man with all the confidence of a man who knew his instructions would have been carried out to the letter.

'It's been brought to an agreement?'

'Yes.'

'Then I want to talk to Miss Childe alone.'

Eve had not moved or spoken. Shock held her rigid while wave after wave of emotion churned up conflicting thoughts. He was Paul Lamarr, not a drifting fisherman. And oh God! She had virtually accused him of being a gigolo, a beach-bum on the make. He had told her that her identity held no attraction and why should it when he was Paul Lamarr.

Had he brought her here to show her that? Ram it down her throat? He looked so much in control. Stay with me ... stay with me ... the words pealed around her brain. What had this powerful man wanted? A part-time mistress for his beach-cabin hideaway? Why had he manoeuvred her into coming here now? To take up where they had left off? Where she had left off. She had walked away. He had not wanted her to go. He had been so angry, contemptuous. And had every right to be. Except he could have told her who he was. He could have settled her fears with a word. But he hadn't. He had let her go with a wave of disgust. And now . . .

The thud of the door closing behind John Lindsey triggered the words which were uppermost in her mind. 'What do you want?' Her voice was sharp, edged with panic.

A quick frown cut a V between the straight dark eyebrows. 'I'm sorry this has been a shock to you. Circumstances change . . .'

'They couldn't have changed more, could they?' She gave a hysterical little laugh. 'The high and mighty Paul Lamarr is putting me in my place. Well and truly.'

The frown deepened. 'It was not my intention to lord it over you in any way.'

'N-no?' The word was a quaver of disbelief. Eve was too blinded by the vast change in circumstances to see the situation any other way.

'No.' The answer was firm, just short of explosive.

There was no further explanation. The dark eyes bored into hers with an intensity which was wholly discomforting. She could feel his power winding around her. He seemed to be waiting for some signal from her and suddenly she was afraid of her vulnerability to this man. Afraid of where it might lead if she revealed how deeply he affected her. In helpless agitation she walked over to the large picture window, turning her back to the disturbing force which was Paul Lamarr.

Her mind clamped on to the job offer and chewed it into meaningful little bits. A trial

commercial. No guarantee of a contract. Unless
Mr Lamarr was satisfied. Satisfied. The word
stuck and billowed with images. He wanted her
back. But on his terms. A powerful man flexing
his power. Maybe he even knew how desperate
she was for work. She had insulted him, walked
away. A man like him, a man used to getting his
own way, snapping his fingers for a woman, any
woman . . .

'It's . . . it's not a real job is it?' She could not
bear to look at him but she had to know the truth.
'You're just dangling out the bait so I'll play
along with you.'

There was an excruciating silence. Her words
hung in the air, vibrating with ugly meaning,
spreading out tentacles which clutched at her
heart, squeezing mercilessly.

'And will you play along with me, Eve?'

The question was soft, yet its overtones struck
her like hammer-blows. There was no sound
from him but intuition screamed that he had
moved up behind her. Her skin prickled with
alarm. She swung around to face him and he was
close, suffocatingly close. Her breath caught in
her throat. Every nerve was electrified by his
nearness.

She opened her mouth to speak but his hand
brushed her cheek in a soft caress and the cry of
protest dried up on her tongue. The insidious
magic of those finger-tips sent a wave of heat
through her body, re-awakening memories she
had tried to erase. Her heart fluttered like a
captive bird. She pressed a hand to it, desperate
to quell its wild tattoo.

The shattering truth burst across her mind, tearing aside all the imposed veils of convention. There was no right or wrong about it. She yearned to feel this man's arms around her again, his body pressed to hers, belonging together as they had in the sea that afternoon, an incredible joining of two people into a unit where nothing else existed.

'The contract is yours, Eve. If you give me what I want.'

His voice was a low, seductive murmur. He moved as he spoke, his hands sliding over her hips, sensuously relearning the curves as he fitted her lower body to his. The hard strength of his thighs made her legs tremble with weakness. Eve could not believe this was happening here and now, in this office, yet intuition told her that this man could make it happen anywhere, and she was mesmerised by her instinctive response to him. Her body had a will of its own and it revelled in the sensations which only he had ever aroused.

He took her handbag. She heard it thud on the floor but the slight noise was strangely distant, over-ridden by the louder thud of her heart-beat. Then his hand was at her waist, underneath the loose tunic-top of her suit. Finger-tips lightly traced the curve of her spine. Up and down, up . . . a shiver of pleasure crawled across her skin. The touch roved further, across her back, under her arm, lingering over the soft swell of her breasts.

Her own hands lifted, instinctively drawn to him. They spread over the fine silk of his shirt, following the contours of the powerful chest she knew so well. Had never forgotten. She felt his

sharp intake of breath and looked up into eyes
which were dark with unfathomable depths. She
did not know that her own eyes were a green haze
of desire, that her lips were parted, quivering
with anticipation. Not until his mouth came
down on hers, harshly plundering, did she even
question the need which had driven all sense of
time, place and circumstances from her mind.

There was a split second of resistance. Then
the violent passion of his kiss sparked an
overwhelming response. Hard hands thrust her
closer, savagely possessive. She melted against
him, exultant in her surrender, revelling in the
rawness of his desire. Her arms wound around
his neck, owning him as fiercely as he owned her.

His fingers thrust roughly through her hair,
clutching her head too tightly for a moment, then
sharply pulling it back. Eve gasped in hurt
protest at the painful wrench. She lifted her eyes
in puzzled appeal and stared disbelievingly at the
blazing anger in his.

'I don't trade business for sexual favours, Eve,
but it's interesting to know how far you'll go for
the sake of your career.' He straightened her
tunic-top and stepped back, sweeping her with a
look of utter contempt.

'I . . . I don't understand you,' she cried. It was
a plea from the heart carrying all the agony of
confusion.

'You couldn't even begin to understand me.'

The coldness in his voice chilled the heat from
her body. She shuddered. Her hands lifted
automatically, rubbing at her arms to restore
feeling. She was completely dazed, unable to

come to grips with the situation.

'Why?' she choked out in bewilderment.

One eyebrow rose with cynical emphasis. 'You think you're irresistible, Eve? You think that because I once found you exciting, you have only to offer me your body and I'll be putty in your hands?' He made a sharp sound of disgust and turned away.

She watched him walk around his desk and settle himself in the comfortable leather chair. His scathing words had whipped away the last trembling traces of desire. He was indeed a stranger now, a cold, unfeeling alien. He sat behind his executive desk, a man of power and authority who did not hesitate over cutting others down to size. He had just reduced her to dirt under his feet.

'Don't underestimate me again, Eve. I don't play with my work. There's nothing I want from you except your professional services as a model. The other directors of the company don't think you can do the job. If you satisfy them, and me, the contract's yours.'

It was a curt statement of fact, completely emotionless. His eyes sliced through her as though she was meaningless fodder for the cameras.

'Why choose me?' It was more an accusation than a question, a spark of defiance rising out of the ashes of her humiliation.

He leaned back in his chair, surveying her with hooded eyes. 'Because you can do the job. I've seen a side of you the others haven't.'

A painful tide of hot blood scorched up her

neck as his words conjured up too many painful memories of how much he had seen of her.

'And strange as it might seem, I wanted to please you,' he added with a savage twist of self-mockery.

'Please me,' she echoed in a strangled voice.

He smiled a thin, pleasureless smile. 'You showed me how much you valued your career when you walked away that afternoon. This contract should set you towards international success. You could say I'm returning a favour. You gave me something I valued. I'm now giving you something you value ... free of charge. All you have to do is perform for the cameras.'

Eve felt sick. The blood drained from her face as the full impact of his words sank in. Too late she recognised that what they had shared together had been of irreplaceable value, a magical affinity so rare that it had seemed a dream. Her own uncertainties and suspicions had ended that dream. A few moments ago it had lived again for her, but not for him. She had poisoned it with rash, frightened words which had risen out of the terrible vulnerability she had felt. There was no way back now. He had judged and condemned her.

'You think I'd sleep with you just to ... to further my career?' she asked in faltering protest even while knowing it could do no good. There was nothing she could do or say which would change his view of her.

His mouth twisted with distaste. 'It's hardly a new idea, is it? Shall we get down to business? I prefer not to waste my time on irrelevancies.'

He waved her to a chair. She took an unsteady step towards it. Her foot knocked against something. It was her handbag, still lying on the floor where it had been dropped. Tears stung her eyes as she bent to pick it up. A wave of desolation accompanied her move to the chair but she concentrated hard on sitting with all the conscious grace of a trained model, her legs folded to one side in the approved sitting position. The only thing she had left to cling to was her career, and it was in a shambles because of her break-up with Simon. It was necessary to swallow her pride and listen to what Paul Lamarr had to offer.

'First let me explain that we're not interested in your professional image. We're after something fresh and original to sell our new perfume.'

Eve showed her puzzlement. 'But if you don't like my work . . .'

'I'm sure you've been very effective but the Lamarr girl has to be all woman, not a provocative teaser.'

Eve blushed a fiery red and was furious with herself for reacting to the label. Paul Lamarr was only stating the truth. The image created by Simon had been a deliberate sexual tease.

'What precisely do you have in mind?' she asked stiffly.

'I want a woman whose beauty is entirely natural, unaffected. A woman with a dream-like quality of innocence. In short,' his voice dropped to a flat monotone, 'I want the woman I saw on a beach one afternoon. If you're a good enough actress to deliver that on film, then the contract is yours.'

Eve was stunned. She had revealed so much of herself that afternoon, believing that her secret inner self was safe with the understanding stranger. She had let herself be a free spirit, uncaring of consequences, and it had been wonderful. To even contemplate commercialising that private magic seemed a monstrous betrayal of trust, yet that was what Paul Lamarr was suggesting. Not suggesting. Demanding.

'You'd ask that of me?' she choked out. It was too much. How dared he be contemptuous of her for supposedly selling her body when he was prepared to peddle her soul for a perfume.

Surprise flickered in his eyes. It was abruptly quenched. 'Aren't you a good enough actress to reproduce that mood?' He turned the question into a deliberate taunt.

She hated him in that moment. Hated him with all the force of her being. She had been mistaken. The feeling had all been on her side. That afternoon meant nothing to him. Perhaps a pleasant interlude. Nothing of value. He had not cared. Did not care. She was a model to be used. That was all it could ever have been for him, a man who had obviously known so many beautiful women. A bleak desolation hollowed out her heart and shadowed her expression.

'Eve . . .'

The harsh demand in his voice barely registered. She looked blankly in his direction, wondering why he had said she had given him something he valued. The answer which sprung to mind brought a twist of irony to her lips. Her virginity. Of course. Didn't men prize virginity in a woman? So odd that it should matter one way or the other. It was only the loving which mattered.

'Eve.'

His voice was more insistent, slicing through her reverie. His eyes had that probing intensity again and he had leaned forward with a tautness in his body she had not noticed before.

'Do you mean . . .' he hesitated, '. . . did that afternoon mean something special to you?'

How could she admit that now? He had made it impossible. Shaming. 'Only in so far as any fantasy is special,' she replied carelessly. 'But if that's what you want, Mr Lamarr, I'll do my best to—how did you put it—reproduce the mood? At least I can try,' she added wryly.

She had to try. If she walked out on Paul Lamarr's offer she would have to admit failure to her mother. And Simon.

'Ah yes! Fantasy!' The words were breathed out on a sigh. Paul Lamarr sank back into his leather chair and relaxed. His mouth curved with grim amusement. 'That's the name we've chosen for our new perfume. Fantasy. I'm sure you'll be able to do it justice, Eve. After all, I know you can make a fantasy . . . almost real.'

Only the most rigid self-control prevented Eve from hurling the job back in his face and walking out. Hatred fired her blood to boiling point but somehow she kept the steam locked in, gritting her teeth with fierce determination. She would show him she was a professional model, all right. She would show them all; her mother, Simon, the whole damned world, but Paul Lamarr most of all. Pride insisted that he never know how deeply he had hurt her.

'I hope you'll be satisfied,' she grated out through her clenched teeth.

'Our first objective is to demonstrate your suitability for the role to my fellow directors,' he said blandly. 'Are you free tomorrow morning?'

'Yes.' There was no point in pretending she was busy.

'Good. I'll arrange a meeting. Be here at nine o'clock. Or is that too early for you?'

'No.'

'You won't need to go to a hairdresser first. I want to present them with the new Lamarr girl so wash out that sleek style and let your hair dry into its natural curls. And please refrain from using any make-up whatsoever.' His eyes skimmed over her in cold appraisal. 'Have you something more obviously feminine in your wardrobe?'

'What would you suggest?' Eve asked tightly. He was stripping her down to the bone.

He shrugged. 'A form-fitting dress perhaps? I want your breasts to be seen. Your photographs tend to make them appear negligible.'

Her control broke. 'Why don't you ask me to prance naked?'

There was a flare of irritation in his eyes. Then his mouth twitched into a sardonic smile. 'Lamarr aims for sensuality and excitement. Women don't appreciate the obvious and my fellow directors are women. I'm sure you can show off your natural attributes without being crudely obvious.'

Eve flushed. His smooth riposte had turned her impulsive jab into a very crude shot. She realised how stupid it was to show her vulnerability. Misdirected pin-pricks were futile. Paul Lamarr had all the big guns in this situation. He did not need her but she needed what he was offering.

'As you wish,' she said flatly, knowing that surrender was the only course to take. 'Is there anything else you would like me to do?' she added with a semblance of sweet reasonableness. She lifted clear green eyes behind which was a steady wall of defence. The surrender was very superficial.

His face seemed to grow harder, all harsh lines and angles. The stab of his eyes was edged with fine contempt. Inwardly Eve returned his contempt, measure for measure, but she kept her gaze limpidly submissive. It gave her a feeling of triumph. He could no longer wound her with his contempt.

'No. There's nothing else I want of you,' he stated with almost insulting precision. 'If you're ready to sign the agreement now, Lindsey can take you along to the legal department.' He leaned forward.

'One thing, Mr Lamarr,' Eve flashed at him before he made contact with the intercom.

He raised questioning eyebrows.

'I understand that this agreement is on a purely professional level?'

'I thought I'd made that eminently clear.'

'Then I insist on being addressed in a purely professional way Mr Lamarr. I resent your familiar use of my personal name. You have no right to call me Eve.'

The dangerous flare in his eyes gave mute warning that her challenge had been foolish. Anger suddenly exploded out of him.

'Just who the hell do you think you are to dictate terms to me?' he thundered at her, exasperation driving his voice up several decibels. 'You don't rate even a glimmer of recognition on the international scene. There's a whole list of women . . . natural draw-cards for this campaign! But I risk time and money to give you your chance at the big-time and what bloody thanks do I get! First you insult my integrity and intelligence. Then your God-almighty ego gets pricked on a few necessary instructions. And on top of that, you have the incredible impudence to stand on your dignity and tell me what I should call you!'

He dragged in a harsh breath and his tone dropped to a low, biting sarcasm. 'Well, hear this, Miss Eve Childe! I'll call you any damned name which comes to mind. You should be thanking your good fortune that you're here to be called anything at all. If you don't like it, get up and keep walking, because in God's name, you are instantly replaceable! You've already cost me more trouble than you're worth. Do I make myself clear, you silly little girl?'

Tears welled up in her eyes and a huge lump of unrelieved emotion constricted her throat. Her brain admitted the damning facts. Looked at from his point of view she had been very silly, but from the moment she had entered this room, Eve had been incapable of any clear focus on the job offer. There had been too many distracting tangents scattering her thoughts.

'I'm sorry,' she choked out. It was barely a whisper and she threw him a despairing look of appeal.

He sighed and ran a hand over his face, casting off the stiff anger. His expression sagged into weariness. 'I'm sorry too. It's no good. It was a mistake bringing you here.'

'No, please. I do want the job and I am grateful for the offer. It was just ... I couldn't ...' she sought helplessly for an explanation, then gave up. 'I'll do my best really I will,' she pleaded anxiously.

For long, taut moments he stared at her in silence. Eve had the forcible impression that he was not seeing her at all, yet he looked directly at her.

'Fantasy,' he finally muttered and his lips curled around the word in soft derision. He seemed to give himself a mental shake and the heavy eyelids came down, reducing his gaze to narrowed slits. 'Well, the agreement is ready for you to sign. Unless you have something else to say we might as well get on with it.'

She shook her head.

He activated the intercom. 'Send Lindsey in.'

The door opened to admit the PR man almost immediately. Paul Lamarr rose to his feet and Eve followed suit.

'Sign up Miss Childe and proceed with the necessary arrangements.' He nodded a dismissal. 'Nine o'clock tomorrow morning, Miss Childe.'

He did not move from behind his desk. He

stood straight and tall, a commanding figure of power and authority. She had been dealt with and now she was being summarily dismissed. Eve drew in a deep, steadying breath and walked over to John Lindsey. He smiled his charming smile and held the door for her. She could not return the smile. It was all she could do to make her retreat with dignity.

It was a retreat in more ways than one. Paul Lamarr's angry outburst had cleared her mind. He held all the cards and she had to play his way if her career was to survive, let alone climb to the top. Maybe it would have been better to go back to Simon, she thought defeatedly, but the more rational part of her brain denied this. The job for Paul Lamarr was a short-term arrangement. It would soon be over. And maybe she would be successful. By herself. For herself. Surely that was worth a bit of heart-ache.

As for the rest, that day she had spent so intimately with him was a closed episode. Far distant, forever locked in another dimension which did not even relate to the present. Yet when he had kissed her ... Forget that, she ordered herself sternly. Paul Lamarr was ... Paul Lamarr. That was the end of it.

CHAPTER SIX

'You're not going like that!'

Eve sighed and threw her mother a look of exasperation. 'Mum, I told you all the details of the proposition. I don't intend to jeopardise this chance by ignoring instructions.'

Marion Childe sniffed her contempt. 'What do men know about presentation? You'll be seeing Margot Lamarr this morning. The queen of cosmetics! She won't expect you to turn up barefaced.'

'It's Paul Lamarr who runs the business, Mum,' Eve reminded her curtly.

'He wouldn't notice a touch of blusher. Or a subtle eye-liner for that matter. A bit of cheating won't go astray,' her mother argued. 'Black's not black and white is certainly not white in the cut-throat world of business. You've got to shade things your way. It's about time you learned that, Eve.'

'I don't think Mr Lamarr appreciates shades of grey, Mum,' Eve said with a touch of irony. She suspected black was very black to Paul Lamarr and cheating would most certainly be black. 'He said no make-up and I'm following his instructions to the letter.'

Marion Childe's lips thinned in disapproval. 'Stubborn,' she muttered as her eyes ran critically over her daughter's appearance. 'Well, at least the dress has style. I hope he appreciates that.'

Eve hoped so too. She had spent all yesterday afternoon searching through boutiques for just the right dress. Pride demanded that Paul Lamarr should find nothing to criticise this morning. It was a pretty, feminine dress and the clinging fabric hugged every curve. The high, rounded neckline was deceptively modest because the overall effect was sensuality personified. The shell-pink of the elongated bodice ran to her hips, tightly form-fitting all the way. The gored skirt featured zig-zag borders of a delicate mauve and a pastel sea-green.

It was a dress which high-lighted Eve's natural colouring. Her silky, blonde curls suited its femininity and the startling green of her eyes was quietly emphasised. She was pleased with her choice. High-heeled, pink sandals added stylish elegance as did the pouched leather handbag which had been dyed to match. The novelty of appearing her natural self secretly delighted her, and to her mind, she looked better than she had for a long, long time.

She said a firm goodbye to her mother, blithely letting all the repeated advice flow over her head. She set off with the lightness of step she had experienced that day on the beach. This morning she was free of the old Eve Childe image. This morning she was herself. The only disturbing factor was the man she was going to meet. Eve knew it was necessary to curb her emotional reaction to Paul Lamarr, yet every time she thought of him it was physical chaos. Her stomach fluttered haphazardly, her skin prickled with apprehension and her nerves played a devastating game of catch-me-if-you-can. As she made her way to the Lamarr building, Eve worked on preparing herself for their meeting, intent on presenting a calm, confident surface.

By the time she arrived in the reception area on the Executive Floor she felt reasonably pleased with her composure. She could even smile at the surprise in the receptionist's eyes. Yet as she was shown into Paul Lamarr's office, her nerves stretched to screaming pitch. He was standing in front of the picture window, apparently oblivious of her entrance. She willed him to turn around, take the initiative, give her some hint of his mood. He did not move.

'Good morning,' she forced out stiffly, determined that he not find her lacking in civility.

Paul Lamarr swung around and immediately his dominating presence projected its aura of power. His eyes swept over her in sharp appraisal. Eve's stomach cramped as she waited for the inevitable comment.

'Good morning,' he nodded, whether from courtesy or approval Eve could not tell. His expression gave nothing away. His gaze lingered on her breasts. 'You're wearing a bra.'

Eve was not sure if it was a statement or a question. 'Yes, of course,' she answered quickly, aware that her pulse had jumped into an erratic rhythm.

'Take it off. You don't need it and my sister will immediately assume it's padded.'

'But ...' Eve mentally cringed at the hard

implacability on Paul Lamarr's face. 'You said not to be obvious,' she finished limply.

'The dress fabric is not transparent. Don't tell me you've never gone without a bra, Miss Childe.'

The cynicism in his voice brought a hot tide of embarrassment flooding up her throat. Paul Lamarr was not going to believe a denial. Eve glanced around helplessly. 'Where can I go?'

'Go?'

'To take it off.'

The dark eyes mocked her request. 'I haven't time to waste on coyness, Eve. Your body holds no secrets from me, as well you know. Take it off here while I check if my mother's ready to receive you.'

A wave of hatred gorged her throat as he turned his back on her and strode over to the desk. How dared he treat her so cavalierly! As if ... as if she was a model, Eve reminded herself savagely. There was no time to waste. Paul Lamarr was already speaking into the intercom. She spun around and dropped her handbag on to the nearest chair. With as much speed as her fumbling fingers permitted she unzipped her bodice, removed her bra, stuffed it in her handbag, then readjusted the dress so that it fitted her snugly.

Her hands were reaching for the zipper again when other, stronger hands performed the service for her. Her skin crawled with sensitivity as his fingers fastened the hook and eye at the nape of her neck. Her body played traitor to her feelings, the nipples of her breasts hardening

and becoming prominent under the clinging
material.

'Ready now?' His voice was toneless, seemingly
disinterested.

Eve furiously cursed her physical vulnerability
to the man. 'Yes, thank you,' she added stiffly,
making a slow business of picking up her
handbag. She willed him to move away but he
was still close to her when she turned around.

Two angry spots of colour burnt in her cheeks.
She lifted her thick eyelashes and glared defiance
at him. It rattled her composure even further to
find an unexpected softness in his eyes. For one
confused moment the office drifted in a haze and
the memory of sea and sand was overwhelming.

'You look . . . very beautiful.' The words were
dragged out, as if spoken against his will.

She caught her breath as he seemed to lean
towards her.

'Eve.'

What was it in his eyes . . . torment . . . desire?
Strong, intense feeling wrapped around Eve,
holding her captive. Every nerve in her body
tingled with anticipation, acutely aware that he
was about to say something vitally important.
Then the moment lost its vibrancy. She felt his
withdrawal before he took the half-step backwards.

'Not the time,' he sighed, and the electric
intimacy was gone like a phantom which had
never existed.

'Come.' He took her elbow and began steering
her towards the door. 'You'll have to maintain
the calm control of a Daniel this morning. You're

about to walk into the lion's den, or rather the lioness's lair. My mother clawed her way to the top and age hasn't blunted her claws,' he added drily.

It was a friendly warning. Eve's confusion grew. She did not understand Paul Lamarr at all. His manner to her now contrasted so sharply to what had gone before that she accompanied him in a dizzy state of puzzlement. His touch on her arm did nothing for clarity of thought either. Despite all the negative emotion he had stirred, he had only to be close to her and she reacted positively to his physical magnetism.

They walked through the reception area to a door, then into another reception area. The change in decor was dramatic, from streamlined modernity to all the elegance of a past age. Eve's high heels sunk into the deeply piled peach carpet. The furnishings were rich and exquisite, velvet and lace curtains, antique furniture, tapestry and polished wood and opulent vases of roses. Even the receptionist's desk was beautiful. Eve's eyes were inevitably drawn to the gold-framed portrait on the far wall. The imperious face of Margot Lamarr was warning enough that she would not suffer fools gladly.

Paul Lamarr murmured a casual greeting to the immaculately groomed receptionist as they moved past. The woman's eyes glowed with interest. Eve was given no time to speculate on relationships. She was steered straight in to an office which could have been the drawing-room in a palace. Or throne-room. Margot Lamarr sat in a high winged armchair behind a magnificent

Chippendale-style table, very much the Chairman of the Board. A second woman sat to the left hand side of the table, her chair turned outwards, towards the newcomers.

Eve was immediately the focus of sharp, speculative eyes. Neither of the two women moved or spoke, but the silence was thick with questions. That they were mother and daughter was obvious. The likeness was startling. Both were large-framed and strong-featured, handsome rather than beautiful with their dark eyes, creamy skin and thick auburn hair. Margot Lamarr's heavier eyelids and slight looseness around the jaw betrayed her age, but the facial bone-structure of both women made age relatively painless as far as looks were concerned.

'Margot Lamarr, Kristen Delaney ... Eve Childe.'

It was more of an announcement than an introduction. It seemed odd that he should put their names on an equal basis without titles to differentiate their positions.

'I'm very pleased to meet you,' Eve said with cautious politeness. Their watching silence had already begun to unnerve her.

'No doubt,' the younger woman muttered waspishly.

'Kristen!' The tone and the glance was reproof enough. Margot Lamarr was accustomed to command. She returned her gaze to Eve. 'I have been looking forward to meeting you, Miss Childe. I can now see that your previous image was very misleading. To be frank, I would never have given you a moment's consideration. But

Paul does sometimes come up with the unusual. Rest assured that you'll now be given fair consideration. You may sit down.'

'Not so fast, Mother. I might have been outvoted but I won't be ignored. We haven't even seen how she moves.'

The resentment in Kristen Delaney's voice sent a tingle of apprehension up Eve's spine. Paul Lamarr left her side and strolled over to the chair on the right hand side of the table. As he settled into it he made a lazy, uninterested gesture to Eve, clearly advising compliance.

'Walk up and down, Eve.'

Her modelling career had been concentrated on the camera. Eve had never experienced the pressures of the cat-walk, eyes dissecting her body in clinical detail as she moved. It was difficult to maintain a pose of indifference in the face of such critical attention.

'Enough!' Margot Lamarr's voice was decisive.

Eve was relieved to come to a halt.

'Well, Kristen?'

Eve glanced towards the younger woman, hoping for a sign of approval. Kristen Delaney's expression lightened but it was a malicious smile which curved her mouth.

'I'd like to see her play out the fantasy. A body is one thing, the ability to project a mood, quite another.'

'Miss Childe has not yet received a script of the fantasy, Kristen. Lindsey has organised a meeting with our film director later this morning.'

The cool statement by Paul Lamarr brought a flare of triumph to his sister's eyes.

'You see, Mother? Not even an audition!'

The old lady's face was as unreadable as her son's. 'Your brother is not a fool, Kristen. No doubt he has reason to believe Miss Childe is capable of performing.'

'He has reason!' The words were tossed out scornfully. 'Well, there's no proof available of that, is there? He's signed this . . .' She waved an airy hand in Eve's direction but disdained to give her the courtesy of recognition. 'This parochial model up for a pilot commercial which is going to cost the company a minimum of twenty thousand dollars, and I say we're entitled to some proof that this investment is not money down the drain.'

She turned to Eve, her dark brown eyes glinting with malice. 'Well, Miss Childe, I'll tell you what we want and you give it to us. You're walking along a beach collecting shells. One of the shells is the Fantasy perfume. You open the bottle, apply the perfume and dream that you're a mermaid who is surprised by a fantasy lover. His kiss turns you into a woman.' She picked up a small box from the table and held it out. 'Here's the perfume. Let's see you put it on and dream. Your face should tell it all.'

Eve's heart had shrunk into a tight ball as Kristen Delaney spelled out the details. Her whole body shrieked a protest. Paul Lamarr was not only demanding that she be the woman on the beach, he was intent on replaying that afternoon with all its personal nuances.

'I can't!' It was almost a sob of protest, a harsh, strangled sound.

'You can't?' Kristen Delaney taunted. 'What do you mean, you can't? It's a reasonable request. Here.' The small black box was offered more insistently. 'Do please get on with it.'

Eve could not look at Paul Lamarr. She glanced at the queenly figure behind the table, hoping desperately that Margot Lamarr might release her from this impossible task. There was no help from that quarter. The dark, obsidian eyes were observing Eve with cold detachment. There was no help from Paul Lamarr either. His continued silence emphasised that she was totally alone in this.

Eve forced herself to step forward and take the perfume. The square black box carried the gold Lamarr emblem. She removed the lid. On a soft bed of peach satin lay a scalloped shell. It was sculptured from plastic but tinted a mother-of-pearl sheen which made it look real. Two seed pearls formed the opening catch. Eve's fingers trembled as they snapped it apart. Inside was a tiny shell-shaped bottle of perfume.

She knew it was no earthly use, unstopping the perfume and dabbing it on. Her eyes lifted to Margot Lamarr, appealing for understanding but expecting rejection. 'I'm sorry. I can't do it. I'm not an actress who can switch a mood on and off. I have to feel it . . . and I can't. Not in this room,' she explained haltingly.

'Oh that's brilliant, that is!' Kristen Delaney scoffed, slapping her hand down on the armrest in disgust while sending a scathing look towards her brother. 'A fine choice, Paul! You've budgeted for two days' shooting. Two days!

What if she can't feel the mood? How far over the budget do you intend to indulge this whim of yours?'

The sneer brought a flush of pride to Eve's cheeks. 'I'll do my best within the time, Mrs Delaney.'

'Your best!' the woman jeered, not the least bit mollified by Eve's tentative assurance. 'And what guarantee do we have that your best is even adequate?' She turned to her mother with a smug air of having settled the matter. 'I don't know how you can tolerate Paul's judgment in this affair. I'll remind you again, Mother, that bringing in an unknown is totally against company policy. When this pilot study fails I expect my opinions to be given more weight. And I'll be demanding some very stringent accountability for this mistake.'

Margot Lamarr arched her eyebrows in haughty disdain. 'Don't presume to tell me what I should do, Kristen. It has yet to be proved a mistake, and it's not good business to allow policies to become stagnant. New blood can be exciting and productive. It could be that Paul has found a star who will give us the advertisement of a decade.'

'A star! Good God! No one outside of Australia has even heard of her. You'll see I'm right, Mother.' She rose to her feet and grew more formidable with all the puffed-up confidence of her rightness. 'Since I've been outvoted on this matter I see no point in staying. I have no doubt that the results of this ill-thought-out foray into the unknown will confirm my judgment. I'll leave you to humour your new star.' She strode over to the door with a sniff of contempt at Eve as she passed.

'Kristen . . .'

The authority in Margot Lamarr's voice was muted but very real nonetheless. She emitted power with effortless ease. Her daughter turned reluctantly, one hand remaining on the door-knob in a gesture of defiance.

'. . . you were wrong about one thing. Miss Childe does have pretty breasts.'

Frustration glared out of the younger woman's eyes. Her lips thinned with the effort to retain control. Then with one venomous look at her brother she wrenched the door open, stepped out and slammed it after her.

Eve lowered her lashes and wished the floor would open up and swallow her, anything to be out of this dreadful scene.

'You shouldn't goad her, Mother.' Paul Lamarr's tone was bland, untroubled. 'It doesn't make for peace.'

'There's no peace with Kristen. She can't see beyond her emotions,' came the flat retort. There was a heavy sigh, a rustle of movement. 'You may sit down, Miss Childe.'

Eve glanced apprehensively at the old lady. Margot Lamarr had settled further into her chair, her head tilted back against the studded velvet. The gleam in the hooded eyes seemed coldly reptilian.

Eve sank into the nearest chair, intensely relieved to have been given that concession. She had felt pinned like a trapped butterfly while

Kristen Delaney had unleashed her weapons in
the fight for power. Eve had been made acutely
aware that Paul Lamarr had put his position on
the line in employing her, but his motives seemed
even more indistinct.

Questions buzzed around Eve's mind. Did he
hope to cement his authority by vindicating his
judgment? Or did he have some real, personal
interest in Eve herself? Nothing seemed clear at
all. Her nerves quivered in anticipation of
another inquisition. Eve had been lacerated by
the cub's claws but the lioness had kept hers
sheathed so far.

'I'm sorry you were subjected to that distres-
sing scene,' she began with smooth civility, 'but
it's as well for you to realise you're very much on
trial. I respect Paul's judgment. I wanted to meet
you simply to see what he sees in you. Having
done that, I find myself intrigued. Where did you
first meet Paul?'

The question slid out, catching Eve completely
unprepared. A swift tide of embarrassment
scorched up her neck and a confusion of painful
thoughts made speech impossible. Her lips tried
to form words but her tongue was paralysed.

Paul spoke. 'I saw her on a beach some weeks
ago.'

Eve gulped at the direct answer. She darted a
desperate look at Paul Lamarr, an agonised plea
for discretion. He was facing his mother, his
expression completely neutral.

'She was as you see her today, Mother, only
her natural beauty was even more evident when I
saw her. Unbelievable and quite entrancing. In

fact, it took me quite some time to identify her as Eve Childe. She would not give me her name and she had no idea who I was until she walked into my office yesterday.'

'Ah!' It was a hum of satisfaction. 'That explains a great deal.' The gimlet eyes returned to Eve. 'Were you expecting to hear from him?'

'No!' Surprise whipped out the negative. 'I thought ...' Eve stopped, the colour draining from her face as quickly as it had risen. The attack from Margot Lamarr was not aimed at Eve's work but at Eve personally. 'I thought it was you who was interested in seeing me,' she finished limply.

There was a protracted silence. Eve marshalled her defences to counter the next thrust but she was unexpectedly given a reprieve. Margot Lamarr turned her gaze on to her son. A tired cynicism drew lines of age on her face.

'I hope you know what you're doing, Paul. Kristen does have a point. It's company time and money you're using.'

'It won't be wasted,' he replied shortly.

She rolled her head back and closed her eyes. 'The pieces fit together. Never take me for a fool, Paul. I've given you a free hand. Go and get on with your gamble. I hope Miss Childe is worthy of it.'

Paul Lamarr slowly unfolded himself from his chair. He walked over to the still figure behind the table and placed a hand on her shoulder. 'I'm not a fool either, Mother,' he said softly.

Her hand reached up and covered his, the beringed fingers clutching tightly for a moment.

She lifted heavy lids and for the first time Eve saw her eyes soften.

'I know what it is to gamble. I've had to do it many a time, and often with everything against me.' She smiled. 'I wish you luck.'

He hesitated, apparently about to say something, then turned to face Eve. They both looked at her and their eyes held the same probing intensity. Eve suddenly perceived the close relationship between mother and son, a kinship of spirits that Kristen did not share, would never share. The daughter had been bypassed for the son, the natural inheritor of his mother's life-force.

Eve felt transfixed under that strong, mutual gaze. It took considerable will-power to rise to her feet and step forward to return the box of perfume.

'Keep it, my dear. I'm sure you'll like it. It's the best we've ever produced.'

Eve was flustered by the gentle tone. 'Thank you. You're . . . you're very kind.'

The old lady sighed. 'There's little room for kindness in the cosmetic business. I hope, very sincerely, that you don't let my son down, Miss Childe.'

'I would be letting myself down even more if I don't succeed, Mrs Lamarr. I shall do my best,' Eve said flatly.

A smile broadened the old lady's mouth. She patted her son's hand in an indulgent way. 'I'm certain you will, my dear. Absolutely certain. You have my best wishes. Both of you. I've seen worse gambles pay off.'

Eve's heart gave a funny little lurch at the

linking of herself to Paul Lamarr. It was done in such an oddly knowing way.

'Thanks, Mother,' Paul Lamarr murmured.

The interview was obviously over. He stepped around the table and took Eve's arm. What would have seemed merely a courteous gesture in other circumstances, now seemed a deliberate reinforcing of a link between them. They walked out of the room together and Eve felt so emotionally disturbed, she did not even question where they were going. The door of Paul Lamarr's office had closed behind them before she began to collect her wits.

'My mother never ceases to amaze me. I didn't expect her to don kid gloves. But since Kristen ran true to form you're probably in urgent need of sustenance,' he added with a wry little smile. 'What would you like; coffee, tea, or a strong draught of alcohol?'

The smile scraped over sensibilities which had been well and truly clawed. The pressures of the last twenty-four hours had mounted inexorably and Eve felt herself abused by them, physically, mentally and emotionally. She stared at the man who had devised the whole torture, outraged that he could calmly smile at her and ask if she wanted a cup of tea.

'You are an out-and-out bastard, Paul Lamarr, and I don't care if you tear up that agreement right now,' she stormed at him.

The smile disappeared and any suggestion of softness which had been on his face went with it. 'A little late for second thoughts, Miss Childe,' he stated coldly.

'A little late in letting me know precisely what you wanted, too,' she hurled back at him. 'Why don't you use the whole damned lot?' Her mouth twisted in contempt. 'But of course, the great Lamarr name wouldn't want anything so obviously crude as intimacy! Oh no! A kiss will suffice, provided it's delivered with bare breasts and passion. Well, if that's the scenario you can forget it. I don't do nude shots.'

'You won't be required to,' came the tight retort.

Eve glared at him, hating his knowledge of her body. She could not bear the memories he had so callously evoked. She swung on her heel and paced away from him, spitting out the hurt in uncontrolled bursts.

'Do all your one-night stands provide inspiration for your work, Mr Lamarr? Is it your customary practice to get the women you bed to replay the ... the mood for you in front of a camera?' She turned, eyes blazing with scorn. 'How low-down crude can you get? To use what I felt that day. To exploit something which was totally private and ...' She stopped. With a stab of anguish she realised that the words trembling on the tip of her tongue were far too revealing.

'And what?'

The soft invitation made her shiver. She was suddenly aware that he was not affronted by her outburst. He was watching her intently, his body poised as if ready to spring at her.

'What did you feel, Eve?' Soft, insidious words, slicing through to her heart.

You know damned well what I felt but I won't

give you the satisfaction of hearing me say it, Eve determined in grimly set silence. He stepped towards her and she tensed. He waved a careless hand.

'If it meant nothing to you, what's all the fuss about?'

'It was private . . . personal,' she declared in resentful protest.

He shrugged, but still there was that watchfulness in his eyes. 'You had no trouble walking away from it. In fact you were relieved that I gave you the opening to manufacture reasons for putting it all behind you. It was easier if I was an out-and-out bastard, wasn't it?'

She flinched at the accusation, knowing it was untrue but unable to find words to deny it with credibility. She had walked away because too much had happened too soon, turmoil following on turmoil, charged with wildly varying emotions. It had been necessary to get back on to some steady plateau, to get everything sorted out and in perspective.

The shock of discovering he had known her identity all along had twisted her perspective. The mistrust she had learnt from Simon's betrayal had still been a very fresh wound, fertile ground for infection. She had not thrown those insults at Paul Lamarr as excuses for her departure. The poison of disillusionment had fed them to her.

'I'm sorry I said those things to you,' she choked out. 'I was terribly wrong. But you . . . you could have told me who you were.'

His mouth curled with cynicism. 'Given you

my name, rank and an itemised account of my wealth? Would you have stayed with me then, Eve?'

Truth whispered from her lips. 'I don't know.'

The dark eyes mocked her savagely. 'You'd already chosen to go back to your career. And now I'm a bastard because I'm not letting you keep that day behind you. I'm dragging it right out in front. So what? Why be so sensitive about it, Eve? You can turn it to good account. A success-hungry model like yourself should not expect to keep her privacy. And as to your personal life, it'll become very public once you achieve your ambition. So why should you quibble now? Success is what you want, isn't it? What you want more than anything else? To be Eve Childe, international model of the year?'

Behind the words was a heightened intensity which set her nerves on edge. He was only an arm's length away and if he touched her Eve knew she would give herself away. And what then? A confusion of emotion ripped through her. She wanted to feel again what they had shared together but this was not the man from the beach. This was Paul Lamarr, a cold, ruthless man.

'Yes, that's what I want,' she agreed in despairing defence.

The tension eased away. When he spoke his voice no longer held a dangerous undercurrent. It was soft with a dull weariness. 'Then there's no argument, is there? You do what the script demands. It should be easy for you. Just dredge it out of your memory.'

The intercom buzzed. Without another word

Paul Lamarr strode to the desk and stabbed his finger on the switch.

'Mr Lindsey is on the line, Mr Lamarr. He says it's urgent.'

'Put him through.'

With Paul Lamarr's attention withdrawn, Eve sagged with the hopelessness of the situation. Tiredly, aimlessly, she stepped over to the picture window and gazed out over the city rooflines, seeing only the painful edges of her thoughts. It had been so simple without names. Just a man and a woman reaching out to each other. The importance she had placed on her name had severed their easy communication, and now the name of Paul Lamarr and all which that encompassed, stood as an insurmountable barrier to ever bridging the chasm between them. If she said she wanted him he would despise her, just as he had despised her yesterday for a response which had been completely natural, instinctive. Any appeal would fall on stony ground.

He had her legally locked into a job which was going to drain her emotions, but if she did not go on with it, what alternatives did she have? Every answer was bleak with emptiness. At least this job could lead to a career.

'Eve!' The call was sharp, peremptory.

She swung around, her feelings carefully guarded.

'Are you available all next week? If not, what days?'

'I'm free whenever you want me,' she answered briefly.

He stared at her for a long moment. Then with

a wry grimace he began speaking into the telephone again. 'It might as well be done as quickly as possible. Check with the Weather Bureau and the Wardrobe Department, then arrange what you can. And Lindsey, you know where your orders come from. In future, you will take no notice of Mrs Delaney's demands until you refer the matter to me.' It was a cutting reproof. There was another pause then, 'Keep me informed of progress and send someone up for Miss Childe.'

He frowned as he put the telephone down and was still frowning when he faced her. 'Eve, should Kristen try to apply any kind of pressure on you directly or indirectly, I want to know. Tell Lindsey if I'm not available. I won't tolerate interference at this stage. Will you do that?'

She nodded.

He smiled but it was a tight, cold smile. 'I have no doubt that you'll make a success of this.'

'I hope so.' It was a husky whisper. Her throat was dry and she had no confidence.

He hesitated then spoke with brusque efficiency. 'Lindsey has the head of the film-crew with him. He'll give you a complete script and a rundown on camera angles. You'll be taken to the wardrobe section for measurements and so on. By the end of the morning Lindsey will have worked out a schedule so you'll know what time's involved.'

There was a knock on the door.

'That'll be your escort.' Again that tight smile. 'No doubt I'll see you on the beach in due course.'

On the beach. Eve felt sick but she did her best to cover her reaction as Paul Lamarr led her to the door. She had been lashed enough by his scepticism. Self-protection demanded that she hide her vulnerability from him. He passed her over to the waiting man with barely a nod.

Eve took a deep breath. Paul Lamarr had dismissed her in all but a professional sense. That left her nothing but to be professional. So be it then, she decided firmly as she walked towards the first practical beginnings of the job ahead of her.

CHAPTER SEVEN

THE moment of truth was fast approaching. The rehearsals had not gone badly but Eve knew that Lloyd Rivers was not impressed with her performance. The rotund film-director had coaxed and prodded and pleaded, then snuffled behind his luxuriant beard at the results of his efforts. His hands had rubbed more agitatedly at the impressive paunch as the blue eyes had gradually lost their sparkle. His final words of praise had lacked enthusiasm. They had been trotted out with synthetic approval. He obviously thought she could do no better.

Eve was not sure of it herself. She knew the beach was inhibiting her. She tried to tell herself it was not the same. Caravans and various other vehicles were parked around the log-cabin. There were people everywhere, busy on their various tasks. John Lindsey danced close attendance, ensuring that no problems arose. Eve had been given courteous attention by all the staff. And Paul Lamarr had stayed away. All she had to do was throw more of herself into the role. But that involved remembering too much. And the memories hurt.

Nan Perkins stood back, her pencil-slim body poised at an uncomfortable angle as she scanned the mirror in front of Eve. She pushed irritably at the wave of strawberry-blonde hair which

flopped over her forehead. The large brown eyes
narrowed in critical judgment. 'I think a deeper
shade of lip-gloss,' she muttered and rummaged
in the make-up box for the right tube.

Eve sat very still, her lips slightly parted while
the beautician applied the gloss with swift, skilful
strokes. Nan Perkins was in charge of costume as
well as make-up and she was extremely efficient.
All the Lamarr people were efficient. The whole
programme had gone ahead like clockwork. In a
few minutes Eve would be dressed ready to shoot
the first scene. She would leave the caravan, walk
down to the water's edge and cameras would
begin to roll.

Nan Perkins drew back and studied the mirror
again. 'That does it. You'll look completely
natural on film.' She glanced at her watch. 'Time
to dress.'

Eve stripped to her briefs. She was not to wear
a bra under the Tee-shirt mini-dress. The
garment was a far better fit than Paul Lamarr's
Tee-shirt but the effect was similar. Instead of a
man's belt she wore a pretty girdle of shells. Her
only other prop was a clear plastic bag containing
a variety of shells which she had supposedly
picked up along the beach.

There was a tap on the door of the caravan.
'Ready, Nan?' It was John Lindsey keeping
everything on schedule.

'Ready!' Nan Perkins gave Eve a friendly pat
on the back and a smile which held satisfaction at
a job well done. 'You look lovely. Good luck!'

'Thanks,' Eve croaked, a lump of nervousness
rising in her throat.

John Lindsey greeted her with a wide grin as she stepped out of the caravan. 'Time to get it in the can. The sun's about to set.'

Eve glanced at the horizon. Sea and sky were bathed in glorious colour. The cameras were to capture the last shimmering hues of the sunset before panning in on Eve as she strolled along the beach. She saw that the film-crew were all at their stations. It was not until she and John Lindsey had begun walking down the sand that she noticed the tall, powerful figure standing next to Lloyd Rivers. Her hand clutched the arm swinging next to hers.

'Forgotten something?' the PR man inquired anxiously.

'No.' Eve drew in a sharp, steadying breath. 'That is Mr Lamarr, isn't it?'

'With Lloyd? Of course. He wouldn't miss the shooting. He's ridden this project all the way.'

Eve's nerves screwed a little tighter. She should have expected him. He had said he would see her on the beach, but his absence up to this point had been one pressure removed. To have to perform in front of him—now—when there was no longer any time for trial and error, produced mind-bending pressure. She could not do it. She had to. She was committed and there was no way out. There was no way she could even ignore his presence. John Lindsey steered a direct line to the two men.

'Eve ...' Paul Lamarr nodded an off-hand greeting, his eyes skimming over her in quick appraisal. 'You look the part. Rivers tells me the rehearsals went smoothly.'

Eve darted a look at the film-director but his attention was on the camera-crew. A self-conscious flush crept into her cheeks. 'They were all right,' she murmured.

'Time to take up position, Eve,' Lloyd Rivers cut in abruptly. 'We might need several takes and I don't want to run out of light. When I give you the signal just take it smooth and easy like we practised. Okay?'

She nodded, avoiding Paul Lamarr's intent gaze.

'And walk up the dry sand. We can't have footprints near the water's edge,' was the final instruction as she turned to go.

She could feel those dark eyes following her. The hand holding the bag of shells grew clammy. The sand dragged at her feet. The memory of that other afternoon was suffocatingly close. She tried to push it away, tried to concentrate on the job which had to be done, but Paul Lamarr was watching her and his presence thwarted any possible attempt to act naturally.

With a dull sense of fatalism Eve took up the rehearsed position where dry sand met the damp graininess left by dying waves. She fixed her gaze on camera three which was to pan in on her face at the critical moment.

'Ready to roll?'

The director's call was answered by each camera-crew.

'Eve?'

'Ready,' she called back. She was as ready as she ever would be, under the circumstances.

'Action!'

Eve forced her legs to move in a relaxed stroll. A wave gently rolled the shell which was her first stop. She bent down, picked it up, held it briefly to her ear to listen to the sea's echo, then dropped it into the bag she was carrying. The Fantasy shell was several paces further on. She pounced on it, tried to project excitement as she opened it. The rehearsed movements were carried out one by one. No fumbling. No mistakes. At last she could close her eyes as she caressed the perfume down the line of her throat.

'Cut! That's a take,' the director confirmed in his unenthusiastic but decisive voice.

It was over. Relief was sending out tenuous threads of relaxation when another voice sliced through them, bringing instant tension.

'Everyone please stay in position. Rivers, a word with you.' It was a harsh, peremptory voice, the voice of command. Paul Lamarr was not pleased.

A sigh of defeat drained Eve of all caring. She stood there listlessly, her fingers idly replacing the perfume stopper. A sideways glance showed the two men in earnest conversation. She knew she had done what Lloyd Rivers had expected of her. He would be assuring Paul Lamarr that the take was as good as any he would get.

'It's not what I want!' Frustration exploding.

'She hasn't got it to give.' Decisive judgment.

Eve dropped her gaze to the Fantasy shell in her hands. The perfume held no magic for her. Only Paul Lamarr had given her the magic she craved and somewhere the spell had been lost, dissipated on the winds of mistrust.

She was unaware of the pathetic picture she made, head bowed, shoulders slumped, one toe drawing aimless squiggles in the sand as she struggled with her inner pain. She was unaware of Paul Lamarr's purposeful approach until his words cut into her heart.

'What in hell do you think you're playing at? Wooden mannequins?'

Her head snapped up as if jerked by a string. His hands fell on her shoulders, strong, impatient hands which swung her around to face him. His mouth was a thin, angry line, his eyes puzzled, probing.

'It doesn't live, Eve. You didn't put any feeling into it. Don't you want to make a success of this?'

She stared at him, her eyes bleak with the memory of what had been lost. Her lips moved in a defensive mumble. 'I told you I wasn't an actress.'

'You don't have to act. All you have to do is remember.' His fingers tightened their grasp, digging into the soft flesh of her shoulders. 'Don't you remember that afternoon, Eve? Wasn't it good?' His eyes burned into hers, demanding that she relive the memory.

'It wasn't real,' she choked out, fighting to counter the turmoil he was provoking inside of her.

'It was real!' he insisted vehemently. 'You were here. On this beach. Paddling through this water. You found a shell and you were in love with the dream of freedom. You can't have forgotten,' he added passionately.

'No,' she whispered, caught up in the emotion which throbbed through his voice.

'Then live it again! Do it for the camera. Isn't that what you love more than anything else?'

Pain twisted across her face. 'Oh God!' she sobbed and tried to wrench herself out of his hold. 'You don't understand,' she begged helplessly.

'What don't I understand?'

She shook her head, blinking back the tears.

'Eve . . .'

The hard urgency in his voice brought a surge of hysteria. 'Let me go! I'll try. I'll try again. But you've got to leave. I can't do it in front of you. Just go away and let me get on with it. Please!'

The wildness of her speech brought a heavy frown to his face. 'I'm affecting your performance?'

'Yes . . . no!' she cried out in confusion, desperate for him to leave but equally desperate not to reveal how deeply he affected her.

His hands gentled their hold and ran caressingly down her arms.

She shivered and shrank away from him. 'Please don't touch me.'

He stared at her, disbelief struggling with some other, stronger emotion which stirred her pulserate into leaps and bounds. 'All right. I'll go,' he said with slow, almost strained deliberation. 'You'll give me what I want, Eve?'

'If . . . if I can.' She could not promise, yet she could not deny the tortured demand of his eyes.

He nodded and turned away, striding back to the film director who was standing patiently near one of his camera-crews, waiting for further orders. They were given with sharp, decisive gestures. Paul Lamarr called John Lindsey to his side. More words were spoken. Then Paul Lamarr was walking up the beach. There was no backward glance. He made straight for the four-wheel-drive Land-Rover which was parked on the grass verge.

'Righto! Let's move everyone!' Lloyd Rivers barked out. 'Get those footprints wiped off the sand, shells back in position, film ready to roll. Come on! Come on! Action stations and fast about it!'

He beckoned Eve over to the dry sand. She moved on leaden feet, still watching Paul Lamarr's departure. The Land-Rover roared into life, turned in a tight circle and headed off up the bush-track to the highway.

'You okay?' the film-director asked softly. He stroked his beard and pursed his lips before stretching them into a wry curve. 'You look a bit shell-shocked if you'll pardon the pun.'

'I'm okay,' she assured him. 'How long have I got?'

'Maximum ten minutes. The light's going fast. We can cut in the sunset from the last take but it's better if we don't have to. Think you can do it?'

'I'll get into place.' There was a limit to her assurances.

Eve spent the time immersing herself in the memories of that one magical afternoon. Fears and doubts were ruthlessly locked away. She did not allow herself to question why she should do this for Paul Lamarr, why she should give him this gift of her inner self. Some deep, basic need in her demanded that he see and understand what she had felt that day.

'Action!'

The word prompted her to move. She felt the inner tensions drift away as the sea-breeze wafted through her hair. She could do it for him. She could feel it now, the heady sense of freedom. Only sand and sea around her ... and there was the shell. Childish delight in its perfection. The sea-roar reverberated through her brain, mingled with the echo of words telling her she was beautiful. And another shell. Pink fantasy. Perfume. Its scent sharpened by salt air. Enticing. Beautiful. Caressing her skin. And the memory of tender hands stroking her, loving her. And she wanted that love again. So much. So very much.

'Cut!'

Slowly, reluctantly, Eve dragged herself out of the self-induced dream. A heavy wave of depression washed over her as reality returned with all its emptiness. Remarks flew around the film-crews. She was vaguely aware of excitement on the air but was untouched by it.

'Get that in the can and hold it with kid-gloves!' Lloyd Rivers roared above the hubbub.

'Sure you don't want another take, Lloyd?' someone yelled.

'Drown that idiot!' the film-director retorted with a laugh. He strode over to Eve and wrapped her in a boisterous bear-hug. 'That was great! Great!' he boomed. 'We'll have this commercial wrapped up in gold if you play it like that tomorrow. Beautiful! Absolutely beautiful!'

Eve flushed with embarrassment and wriggled out of his arms. 'I'm glad you liked it,' she muttered.

'Liked it! My God! It sent shivers up my spine.' His grin faded as he sensed her detachment from his jubilance. 'Hey ...' he breathed softly, 'you're not feeling so good, are you?'

She shrugged. 'I'm not an actress. The feeling has to come, and now I'm tired. If it's all over for now, I think I'll go up to my caravan.'

'I'll take you up,' he offered, quick to pamper her needs now that she had proved worthy of special attention.

'No. I'd rather go alone, and you must have work to finish up here,' she added tactfully.

'As you like,' he agreed with an easy shrug.

Eve turned to go but his hand suddenly snaked out to stop her. She glanced back at him questioningly.

'Mind telling me something?'

The curiosity in his eyes sparked a defensive wariness. 'That depends on what it is.'

'I've been in this game a long time and I'm no fool at my job,' he stated matter-of-factly. 'I know how to get the best out of the material I have to work with. This afternoon I used up my whole experience on you and you gave me only the mechanics. Nothing more. Not even a glimmer of the response Paul Lamarr got out of you. So what did he say? I'm always ready to learn new tricks.'

'Ask him,' she said more curtly than she meant to.

His eyes narrowed speculatively. 'He's not a man I care to cross.'

A wry smile curved Eve's lips. 'I guess I don't care to cross him either. Thanks for your forbearance. And I hope I can please you tomorrow.'

He let her go without further comment but Eve was not allowed to go alone. John Lindsey fell into step with her.

'Lloyd sounded pleased,' he remarked with his easy charm.

'Yes.'

'He obviously got what he wanted.'

'What Paul Lamarr wanted,' Eve corrected flatly.

They trudged a few steps in silence.

'You sound a bit down. Anything I can do for you, Eve?'

She threw him a weary glance. 'No. I just want to change out of these clothes and go to my caravan. Be alone for a while. Does that have your approval?'

'It's not a question of my approval,' he protested. 'I simply want to ensure that . . .'

'That there are no problems. I know,' Eve sighed. 'Well, he's got what he wanted so there's no problem. I just have to live with it, that's all.' Tears filmed her eyes, turning them into a green haze of pain as she turned to the PR man. 'And you know what the worst of it is? He doesn't even know what he's got.'

John Lindsey's face was a caricature of incomprehension. He gestured his frustration. 'If you'll explain . . .'

They had reached Nan Perkins' caravan. Eve dashed the moisture from her eyes and took a deep breath. 'It doesn't matter. Take no notice. I'm only maundering. Put it down to the artistic temperament. Please leave me alone now.'

Before he could say any more Eve opened the caravan door and stepped inside. Nan Perkins was not there. Eve quickly changed into her own clothes, put the mini-dress on a hanger in the cupboard and was about to leave when the beautician came hurrying in.

'Sorry! Didn't realise you'd come up. Need any help?' she asked breathlessly.

'No, thank you. I put the dress away. I was just going.'

'Are you all right, Eve? John thought you might need company. I'll come along with you if you like. A chat might help you wind down. Even old hands like ourselves rarely see a performance like that.'

Eve could not help a dry smile. 'Does John Lindsey always fuss around like a mother hen?'

Nan Perkins returned the smile. 'You can't blame him. I've never seen Mr Lamarr so uptight. Of course, Mrs Delaney would love to see him fall flat on his face over this project. That bitch has . . .' She paused as if suddenly realising she had been indiscreet. 'Well, never mind Company politics. And congratulations! Lloyd's walking around with his stomach puffed out and everyone's terribly pleased. We all respect Paul Lamarr. And like the way he runs the Company. His sister is a bitch,' she added feelingly.

'I can't say I cared much for Kristen Delaney either,' Eve commented. 'Thanks for the offer of company, Nan, but I really would prefer to be alone.'

'Okay. I'll see you at dinner then.'

Eve hesitated. Dinner was to be served in the log-cabin. She cringed at the thought of sitting in there for any length of time. Her memories had been brought too close to the surface. 'I think I'll make myself a snack in the caravan and go to bed early. Will you make my excuses to the others please, Nan?'

A frown creased the other woman's forehead as she peered anxiously at Eve. 'Sure you're all right?'

'Yes. Don't worry. I'll be fine tomorrow.' She threw a reassuring smile over her shoulder as she stepped outside then shook her head at John Lindsey who was hovering near the log-cabin.

The caravan which had been supplied for her private use stood at the back of the cabin to the left of the water-tanks. She climbed into it and shut out the world with a vast feeling of relief. The cupboards and refrigerator had been provisioned. There was no need to face anyone this evening, no need for polite smiles and pretended interest. She could indulge herself to her heart's content, only there was no contentment in her heart.

The caravan had a comfortable double bed. She crawled on to it and buried her head in the pillows. The tears she had repressed were given free flow and they flowed for a long time, great welling tears, pushed out by surging waves of misery.

The knock on the caravan door was an intolerable intrusion. Eve dragged a pillow over her head and ignored it. To hell with them all, she thought rebelliously. Whatever was wanted could wait until tomorrow. She had done all that was required of her today. A sharper rap carried impatience and insistence but Eve stubbornly clung to silence.

'Eve, I know you're in the caravan. Either you open the door or I'm coming in anyway.'

A chill ran through Eve's blood. That was Paul Lamarr's voice. But he had gone. She had seen him leave. How could it be his voice? Unless he had come back to check on her performance. But Lloyd Rivers would have reassured him so what did Paul Lamarr want now? Hadn't she given him enough of herself today?

'Eve, I'm coming in.' Hard. Purposeful. Relentless.

'No! Wait!'

Panic shot her off the bed. She couldn't let him see her like this, tear-stained, dishevelled, her defences in tatters.

'I'll only be a minute. Please wait,' she called out, concentrating fiercely on pulling herself together.

She whirled over to the sink, slapped her face with water and briskly towelled it dry, hoping to put colour in her cheeks. Suspecting that he would not give her time to change out of her crumpled clothes, she straightened them as best she could, ran a brush through her hair, took a deep breath and stepped over to the door. No sooner had she pushed it open than Paul Lamarr was brushing past her.

She pulled the door shut after him and immediately berated herself for not having the presence of mind to get out of the caravan. Paul Lamarr dominated its small space and he was too close to her, suffocatingly close. In a bid to minimise his disturbing presence she slid into one of the bench-seats behind the table and only fluttering a side-glance in his direction, gestured an invitation for him to take the opposite one.

'Please sit down, Mr Lamarr.'

The words were stiffly polite, too obviously ill-at-ease and he made no move. Eve was forced to look up at him. The dark eyes burned into hers, anxiously probing. She swiftly lowered her lashes, speaking quickly in an attempt to hide her inner agitation.

'Why did you want to see me? We've finished for the day. Mr Rivers was satisfied with the last take.'

'More than satisfied,' came the soft reply. 'Why are you so upset?'

'I'm not upset,' she flashed back resentfully. 'I'm tired. That's all.'

She could not hold his disturbing gaze without giving away the lie and she would not accept the humiliation of the truth. She stared down at the table.

'Rivers, Lindsey, Nan Perkins, they all said the same thing. You're wound up tight. Too tight. Not the usual reaction to success, Eve.'

Anger rose to the insidious taunt and flared off

her tongue before she could stifle it. 'I did what you wanted. I haven't wasted your money. What do you want now? Just say it. Say it and leave me alone.'

Was it merely the reflection of her own agonised eyes in his? For one vivid moment they seemed to be one again and Eve was tempted to reach out and beg him to understand. The need to recapture what they had once shared hammered through her body and he seemed to be generating the force behind the feeling. But no . . . no . . . it couldn't be so. Not after all he'd said and done. Eve wrenched her gaze away, and lest she be drawn into some weak stupidity, she propped her elbows on the table and covered her face with her hands.

'Eve . . .'

Was it a plea? The rough urgency in his voice suggested it might be so but she could not let herself believe it. She heard the sharp intake of breath and the whisper of a sigh before the touch came on her shoulder. She automatically shrank from it, remembering all too well how he had reviled her for responding to him that first morning in his office. The touch was withdrawn.

'Eve, if you don't want to go on with it. If what I've asked is . . . if it's hurting you, I'll release you from the contract. It wasn't my intention to hurt you, Eve.'

The soft, caring words bit into her heart, painfully recalling the man he had been on the beach. Fantasy, she reminded herself. This could only be compassion for the emotional strain he had inflicted on her. Tears pricked her eyes but

she resolutely forced them back. Dear God! She
didn't want to go on with it but what else could
she do now? Where was she to go? Back to her
mother and Simon and admit failure?

'I have no other choice. I must go on with it,'
she choked out despairingly.

His silence shrieked along her nerves. Go
away, go away, she cried in wordless torment. At
last he spoke, and his voice sounded as strained as
Eve felt.

'I'm sorry. I didn't mean to place more stress
on you by this visit. I only wanted to ... to let
you know there would be no question of
demanding recompense if you wished to walk out
on the contract. I hope it goes well for you
tomorrow.'

Then he was gone, the caravan door rattling on
the emptiness he had left behind. Eve felt like a
hollow shell, as if he had taken her life-force with
him. Why had he softened? What had made him
regret tying her into this contract which he had
planned so ruthlessly?

Eve shook her head in hopeless confusion. She
would never understand why he had done
anything, why he had even bothered to save her
from the sea. At least death was peaceful, she
thought grimly. But so very final, the voice of
sanity whispered, and while there was life there
was always hope of something good turning up
... sometime.

She dragged herself up, made a pot of tea and
cut some cheese on to biscuits. The crumbs had
to be washed down her throat but she munched
on. There was no point in making herself faint

from lack of sustenance. She had to get through tomorrow. Paul Lamarr would have the commercial he wanted. Kristen Delaney would have to admit defeat. And Eve . . . she would have her career, her meaningless, empty career, full of bright lights and inner darkness.

She undressed. The night air had turned unexpectedly chill. With a little shiver she pulled on a nightie, snapped off the light and climbed under the blankets. She turned the damp pillows over and settled herself comfortably. Still sleep would not come. She opened a window and listened to the soothing drone of the sea. It should have soothed her but it didn't. She tossed and turned, her body restless with too many frustrated yearnings.

She heard the muted voices of other people going off to bed. In an attempt to block out disturbing thoughts she concentrated on picking out the sounds of nature; the hum of insects, the intermittent bird-calls, the rustle of leaves. Eventually sleep stole over her but it was full of shadows, nameless, frightening things which tormented her subconscious and gave her no rest.

CHAPTER EIGHT

EVE woke, tired and listless. A buzz of activity told her the day had begun outside. The final scenes of the commercial would not be shot until after sunset but preparation for those crucial minutes would go on all day. Eve dreaded those few minutes. They loomed ahead of her like another nightmare.

Once she had dreamt of being a star, famous, fêted by other celebrities, admired across the world. She had never dreamt of the price that had to be paid for stardom, the sheer personal cost which stripped her life of the privacy she valued. It was too high a price. To perform what had to be performed this evening would leave her emotionally barren.

She could not do it. Would not. Paul Lamarr would have to be satisfied with less than he wanted, even if it meant she forfeited her chance of a contract. She did not want a contract with him anyway. His presence always brought pain and confusion.

'Eve! Breakfast in twenty minutes. Are you awake?' It was John Lindsey, rounding up his wayward chick for the main event.

'Yes. I'll be out in time,' she called back, resigning herself to the inevitable.

She brooded through breakfast, eating little so as to be out of the log-cabin as quickly as possible. She took her coffee outside to where some folding chairs had been set up under the trees. John Lindsey joined her, his forehead puckered with concern.

'Are you all right, Eve? You look a bit pale this morning.'

'No make-up,' she smiled, not wanting to discuss how she felt.

He did not respond to her smile. His eyes scanned her worriedly. 'Any problems I can deal with?'

She avoided his intent gaze, looking past him to the sparkling sea. 'No. It's a lovely morning, isn't it?'

He sighed and dropped into the chair next to her. 'Should be a lovely day. If all goes well.'

Eve sipped her coffee while John Lindsey checked over the work programme with her, making sure she knew where she was expected to be and when. It was an unnecessary exercise but Eve let him talk on, preferring the conversation to be impersonal. Eventually she excused herself to change for the morning rehearsals.

The mermaid scene required her to be in the water. Eve pulled on a comfortable maillot. It was cut high on the thighs for easy leg movement and while it had no real support for her breasts, the stretch fabric held them firmly. She hesitated over a beach-coat then decided it was useless. The sun was already warm and once rehearsals began it would have to be discarded anyway. She picked up a large beach-towel and returned to John Lindsey.

The burr of an approaching vehicle had drawn

his attention. Eve followed his gaze and immediately tensed as Paul Lamarr's Land-Rover bounced around the last turn of the rutted track.

'That'll be Halliday now.'

Eve glanced sharply at the PR man. 'Not Mr Lamarr?'

He threw her a curious look. 'The Land-Rover's a Company vehicle. Were you expecting Mr Lamarr this morning?'

'No. I . . . No.'

She shook her head and once again took refuge in looking out to sea, fiercely telling herself to put Paul Lamarr out of her mind. It was impossible. The whole environment conspired to remind her of him. However, by the time the Land-Rover pulled up beside them she had succeeded in masking her inner tension.

Eve recognised the driver as John Lindsey's man from the PR Department. His passenger alighted with all the cocky confidence of a man who was used to and expected adulation. He filled the tall, dark and handsome mould in every category; lustrous black curls, flashing eyes, white, white teeth, and a body which had been poured into skin-tight jeans and Tee-shirt, all the better to show off the very male muscularity of his undeniably splendid physique.

His eyes gloated down Eve's body and up again. One wickedly arched eyebrow accompanied his opening remark. 'You're Eve Childe? The legs I recognise but the body and face are something else again. The nymphet has definitely turned into a delectable woman. Something tells me I'm going to enjoy being your lover.'

Never, Eve flung at him silntly. She was repulsed by the blatant ego of the man and even more repulsed by the thought of being intimately handled by him.

John Lindsey performed the formal introduction. Eve nodded coolly and very pointedly turned her attention to the conversation between the two PR men.

'Any messages?'

The driver shook his head. 'I have to get straight back. I've got some news for you though. I'll be driving out this afternoon with none other than the old lady herself.'

'Margot Lamarr?'

'And Mrs Delaney. They're both coming.'

There was a short speculative silence which was broken by Rick Halliday, preening himself with self-importance. 'The ladies obviously want to see the action, and there's no way I'm going to disappoint them. Nothing like a V.I.P. audience to get the adrenalin running.'

'Well, it seems you'll have it,' John Lindsey said blandly, but his eyes darted anxiously at Eve for her reaction.

Her carefully impassive face revealed none of the nervous tension which had just tied another knot in her stomach.

'Thanks for the tip-off, Dave. Be sure to give the ladies a very smooth trip.'

'No worries,' the driver grinned. 'It's not every day I get to be the Queen's chauffeur. Be seeing you.'

He climbed back into the Land-Rover, gave a jaunty wave and was off. John Lindsey sighed with some feeling, then turned back to his two charges. Before he could say anything a shout from the beach demanded their attention. Lloyd Rivers was beckoning them down.

Rick Halliday draped his arm around Eve's shoulders and leered at her. 'No rest for the wicked. Let's go, baby.'

Eve stiffened. Her initial antagonism deepened to loathing. This obnoxious man was to play her fantasy lover! The whole concept now seemed doubly impossible. How could she pretend any positive feeling at all when her whole body was screaming negatives?

'We're not rehearsing yet, Mr Halliday,' she said coldly and shrugged off his arm. She fixed her gaze on Lloyd Rivers and strode ahead, kicking the sand with angry feet.

Rick Halliday quickly caught up with her, completely unabashed by her coolness. 'This is our big chance, baby-doll. World-wide circulation! And am I going to make the most of it. Rudolph Valentino, here I come!'

And the awful part was, he took himself seriously. He really did think he was the world's greatest gift to women and his conceit extended into the rehearsals. His attempt to turn the kiss in the mermaid scene into a full-scale assault on her mouth made Eve shudder with revulsion.

'No time for all that, Halliday,' Lloyd Rivers cut in drily. 'Make it short and sweet. We're not running to a full-length movie. Let's just get the action flowing. Finesse can come later.'

It took considerable practice to get the second scene timed correctly. Having been lifted from the water and kissed, Eve had to push away from her lover, dance a few steps to show the joy of having legs instead of a tail, perform an ecstatic pirouette, then rush back to her lover for the final, exultant lift into the air and slide-down embrace. Rick Halliday made the most of that slide-down embrace. His hands relished the exploration of every curve. By the time Lloyd Rivers was satisfied with the routine, Eve was sickened by their lecherous touch.

'Lunch and rest now.'

The words were a welcome release. Eve picked up her beach-towel and wrapped it around her. She felt cold right through to her soul.

'Eve, walk up with me,' Lloyd Rivers ordered rather than invited.

She fell into step beside him, stonily silent.

The film director puffed along, finding the dry sand hard going with the weight he had to carry. His slow progress ensured that the rest of the company was soon out of earshot.

'Eve, if I thought I was going to shoot that sequence as you just played it, I'd walk into the sea and drown myself. I've let it pass because you've got the mechanics right. But I'm telling you now, if you don't come up with the feeling when we shoot this evening, we've got dead film. And all the magic of yesterday will be wasted. You do appreciate that?'

'Yes.'

He glanced sharply at her, not liking the brief answer. 'This is important to me, Eve. A man gets tired of making hum-drum commercials even if he makes them well. This is something special. Can you reproduce the mood?'

They were Paul Lamarr's words. Empty,
meaningless words, asking the impossible. She
had only had one lover. Alone she might have
been able to relive those intense emotions which
the fantasy required. But with Rick Halliday . . .
never!

'I can try,' she answered evasively.

Lloyd Rivers showed his frustration by pulling
up and frowning heavily at her. 'There's time for
more rehearsals this afternoon.'

'No. No more.' Her tone was too emphatic for
any argument. She tried an appeasing smile to
gloss over her sharpness. 'It wouldn't serve any
purpose. As you said, I've got the mechanics
right.'

'Yeah! The mechanics!' he said disgustedly and
gave a defeated sigh. 'Well, play it your way. God
knows it seems I have no say in it.'

They had almost reached the log-cabin. Eve
excused herself and sought the balm of solitude
in her caravan. At least there she was free of
questions and Rick Halliday could not bother
her. She stripped and washed herself clean, made
some lunch, ate it without appetite, then lay
down on the bed.

Sheer weariness dragged her into sleep. It was
deep and dreamless. An insistent call demanded
that she climb out of it but her subconscious did
not want to respond. She clung on to the dark
nothingness until someone was shaking her
shoulder. Her head swam with reluctance but she
opened her eyes. For a moment she felt
completely disorientated, but then she recognised
the woman who stood over her and reality swept

back with a vengeance. She groaned and turned over.

'Sorry, Eve, but you'll have to get up now,' Nan Perkins warned kindly. 'We don't want to run short of time.'

Eve heaved herself off the bed and headed for the sink. She splashed water on to her face, had a quick drink, then gestured her readiness to Nan Perkins.

'You look wrecked,' the woman said sympathetically, 'but we'll soon do something about that. Didn't you sleep well last night?'

'Too restless,' Eve explained shortly.

'Too worked up,' came the knowing comment. 'Never mind. It'll be all over today. Let's get on with it.'

Nan stood guard at the laundry door while Eve showered and shampooed her hair. She hurried the ablutions. There were too many memories here, just as there were in the main room of the cabin. She wrapped herself in the towelling beach-coat then accompanied Nan to her caravan.

In contrast to yesterday there was much to be done. Eve's hair was more carefully arranged into its soft curls. Her fingernails and toenails were varnished a pearly pink. After that, the make-up; a delicate blusher on her cheeks which gave her skin a luminous quality, frosted pink on her lips, and an other-worldly emphasis given to her eyes. A tiny sprinkling of glitter highlighted the arch of her eyebrows. Deep, sea-green shadow on her lids gradually faded to the lightest suggestion of silver-green above her eyes. Below the lower lashes the silver-green was repeated, along with a few minute touches of glitter.

Fitting Eve into the mermaid costume took considerable time. First there was the foam-rubber padding to fill out her legs to a smooth tapering shape. The tail itself was moulded from plastic which was rolled on and pulled snugly to her hipline. With her lower body turned into that of a mermaid, the final costume could be drawn on.

Constructed from a stretch fabric, the tail section was heavily sequinned to give the effect of gleaming green scales. Once it passed the hipline, a finer, transparent fabric formed the bodice. It was flesh-coloured and barely visible. The sequins of the tail became less and less concentrated until only a modest sprinkle high-lighted the rounded thrust of Eve's breasts.

The last adornment was a pendant necklace. Tiny miniatures of the pink Fantasy shell were threaded on a silver chain with the full-size perfume container as a central pendant. This was Eve's one prop for the mermaid scene. She was to finger it dreamily until her fantasy lover surprised her.

'Now you look fantastic!' Nan grinned at her, having taken stock of the finished product.

Eve lay on a dust-sheet on the floor, feeling like a stuffed turkey which was destined to be fed to the lions, or rather, lionesses. Nan had reported the arrival of Margot Lamarr and Kristen Delaney some ten minutes ago. Paul Lamarr had not been mentioned and Eve had not asked about him. She did not want to think of Paul Lamarr.

She did not want to think of anything. She just wanted this whole thing finished, behind her.

John Lindsey knocked and entered. 'Ready to go?' His eyes glinted appreciation as he took in the fairy-tale quality of Eve's mermaid. 'That costume is a work of genius, Nan. Sexiest damned thing I ever saw. No offence, Eve,' he added quickly.

'No doubt it'll help get me through this first scene,' she answered drily.

He beckoned outside and the driver of the Land-Rover climbed into the caravan.

'Wowee!' the younger man goggled at her. 'Maybe I ought to take up fishing.'

'Enough of that!' Nan Perkins laughed, pleased with their reactions to her work. 'You tear off one sequin as you carry Eve down and I'll have your heads.'

With Nan directing the operation the two men picked Eve up, manoeuvred her outside and carried her down the beach.

Lloyd Rivers detached himself from Rick Halliday, shouted orders at the camera-crews and set about directing Eve's exact positioning at the water's edge. He had obviously been watching the run of the waves. Eve was placed so that her tail was just lapped by the water. He checked her pose, moved her supporting arm a little further out so that she was sitting with more of a lean, then waded to the camera platform to make sure that the angle was exactly right.

Eve did not glance around. She had seen the watching group which stood outside the camera-lines but it was easier to pretend it had nothing to do with her. People moved around her, washing out foot-prints. Lloyd Rivers came ploughing back. He stood over her, a grim look of determination on his chubby face.

'Well, it's up to you, my girl. You look gorgeous enough to stun the viewers anyway, but I want more than that. You've got five minutes to think yourself into the role. For God's sake, do it!'

Eve's fingers sought the Fantasy shell which hung around her neck. She stared out to sea, trying to blot everything from her mind, all the twisted, painful thoughts which had tormented her. Gradually the sea rolled over them, the primitive, powerful force of nature which dominated all horizons.

'Action!'

But the sea was empty. She needed something, someone to share the emptiness of her world. Someone to bring her alive. There was so much feeling in her aching to be let out, given, shared, waiting only for the right touch.

The touch when it came was of hot, grasping hands, lifting her up to a hot, demanding mouth which determinedly invaded hers. Instinctively she struggled, frantically pushing at hard, muscular shoulders, bending her head back, fighting desperately to escape that loathsomely questing mouth.

'Cut!'

She kept clawing her revulsion even as he thrust her back.

'You bitch!' Rick Halliday snarled down at her. 'You've ruined the whole bloody scene! What in hell were you fighting me for?'

'Shut up, Halliday!' Suddenly Lloyd Rivers was there, taking her into his arms, supporting her with a gentleness which was in total variance to the sharpness of his order.

'It wasn't my fault!' Rick Halliday protested angrily. 'She came at me like a hell-cat. God! You'd think I was trying to rape her or something.'

Eve shuddered and hid her face against the wide expanse of shirt above Lloyd Rivers' paunch. 'I'm sorry,' she mumbled.

She received a comforting pat on the head. 'Don't you worry about a thing,' the film-director assured her softly. 'We can edit that last bit out. The rest of it was brilliant. Brilliant! That's all that matters for now. We'll go on to the next scene.'

Tears swam into her eyes. 'I can't do it. I can't,' she choked out.

His arms tightened around her. 'Yes, you can. You've got to do it. God! A woman who can emote as you just did can do anything. Now you just calm yourself down while Nan Perkins gets you ready for the finale.' He ruffled her hair in a tender gesture of encouragement then raised his voice. 'Lindsey! Get moving! And handle with care. This is valuable merchandise.'

Eve was once more carried over the beach. She shut her ears to the babble of voices around her. Fortunately John Lindsey and his helper had the tact to remain silent. They laid her carefully on the dust-sheet in the caravan and swiftly departed.

Nan Perkins set to work, quickly stripping off

the sequinned outer garment. Eve helped her roll the plastic tail down and remove the padding. It was a physical relief to be free of that uncomfortable constriction but there was no relief from the ordeal which stretched ahead of her.

With quick, efficient skill Nan repaired and touched up the intricate make-up on Eve's face. Then she held the sea-green dress while Eve stepped into it. Bikini briefs were stitched on to the hipline where a band of sequins supported the filmy, chiffon skirt. The bodice was an exact replica of the mermaid costume so that the transformation from sea siren to woman had visual continuity. Nan repositioned the shell necklace and Eve was ready for the final scene. Ready as far as all outward appearances were concerned. She would never be ready to respond to Rick Halliday with the emotion expected of her.

John Lindsey escorted her back down the beach. Eve darted a nervous glance at the V.I.P. group. Margot Lamarr was speaking to Lloyd Rivers. Kristen Delaney was chatting to Rick Halliday who was wearing a very smug smile. Eve winced and let her eyes skate over Paul Lamarr. He stood slightly aloof from the others and she knew he was watching her approach. Lloyd Rivers tapped Halliday's shoulder and broke away from the group, relieving Eve of the necessity to meet and speak to anyone.

He met her, wrapped his big hand around hers and squeezed it in a conspiratorial fashion. 'One more effort, Eve. That's all we need. We'll pick it up from where you were pushing at Halliday's shoulders. The camera will run down your body to capture the moment when your toes hit the sand. Then up again, and your body has to look pliant, yielding, for that one long shot before you break away.'

'No kiss,' Eve demanded stonily.

Lloyd Rivers took note of the rebellious storm in her eyes and made the concession without argument. 'No kiss. We'll turn you three-quarter on so that it need only be simulated. That won't throw you off?'

Eve dropped her lashes, unable to answer the anxious question in the film-director's eyes. 'It'll help,' she muttered.

They had walked down to the water's edge. Eve was in position for the final shoot. Lloyd Rivers patted her hand. 'Wait here. I'll get Halliday sorted out. We'll have one brief practice of that embrace and then we'll shoot. Okay now?'

She nodded.

It was several minutes before he was back. Eve had not watched him. She did not want to look at Rick Halliday . . . or anyone else.

'All right. Now let's get this embrace looking smooth.'

Eve sensed Rick Halliday's hostility before she turned around. His hands gripped her waist too tightly. She followed the director's instructions as best she could, trying to ignore the revulsion she felt.

'Relax, you silly bitch!' The words were a venomous hiss and his fingers dug cruelly into her flesh.

'Shut your mouth, Halliday, and keep it shut!' came the harsh rebuke. 'Do your part precisely as I said, and Eve will do hers. I'll give you a countdown, Eve, so you can be prepared. Once I call action, you have to give.'

They were left alone. Rick Halliday glared after the retreating figure of the film-director then looked down at Eve with hot contempt.

'You know what you need,' he jeered at her. 'You need someone to grind you into a bed until every last bit of ice is melted. And oh man! Would I love to do it!'

'Five. Four. Three.'

Eve placed her hands on his shoulders and began pressing away from him. Rick Halliday took the opportunity to ram her lower body into his as he lifted her up.

'Two. One . . . action!'

There was no way Eve was going to be persuaded into a repetition of this scene. Spurred on by that thought alone, she carried through the routine action-perfect.

'Cut!'

'Get your hands off me this instant!' Eve snapped at Rick Halliday, her eyes fiercely rejecting him.

His hands slid around with slow insolence and flipped across her breasts as she drew away from him. She barely restrained herself from flying at him tooth and claw.

Lloyd Rivers came charging in, shouting orders in readiness for a replay. He strode up to Eve, heaving dissatisfaction. 'Well, what else do you want? That was useless! You know damned well it was useless! You've got to put that feeling into it. So what's the problem now? There's no point in your giving me that mechanical doll again.'

'That's all you'll get,' Eve bit out angrily, too churned up to even consider his words. She turned on her heel, blindly intent on escape.

Lloyd Rivers caught her arm and swung her back. 'Are you mad? You can't throw it all away! We're two-thirds there. Just one more effort from you and——'

'I won't do it!' she cried wildly.

'You won't do it?' Lloyd Rivers repeated incredulously. He took hold of her shoulders and shook her as he thundered, 'By God! You will do it! We'll shoot that scene again and again until whatever it is inside you cracks and I get what I want. You're under contract, my girl!'

'I won't have that load of slime touch me again! And get your hands off me!' she screamed, flinging off his grasp.

'What the hell . . .'

'What's the trouble?' Paul Lamarr's voice cut in with sharp authority.

Lloyd Rivers threw up his hands in disgust. 'The trouble is she's throwing a temperament fit and won't see sense!'

'Sense!' Eve shrilled. 'There's no sense in continuing. If that filthy gorilla comes near me again, I'll vomit!'

'Halliday?'

She swung on Paul Lamarr, almost beside herself with fury. 'Yes, Rick pig-almighty Halliday! Your marvellous choice of a fantasy lover, who's so damned full of himself that fantasy's not good enough for him! Oh no! Full-scale sexual assault is his style, and if you think I'm going to let him paw me again . . .'

'Now look here, you stuffed-up little snob! If you . . .'

'That's enough, Halliday,' Paul Lamarr directed sternly.

'I haven't even started. She's been pulling against me from the word go. Tell him, Rivers! She isn't even professional enough to do a kiss.'

'You'd have to be a professional whore to stomach your kisses,' Eve spat at him.

'Why you . . .'

'I said enough!' There was no arguing with that steely tone. Paul Lamarr raised his voice. 'Lindsey, over here!'

The PR man hurried forward, closely trailed by Kristen Delaney.

'See that Mr Halliday leaves immediately. Halliday, we no longer require your services. You'll be paid the agreed fee.'

'Now just a Goddamned minute . . .'

'Immediately!'

'Why is he to leave?' Kristen Delaney demanded.

'It's my decision, Kristen. Don't interfere. Please go, Halliday. There is no percentage in arguing.'

'All right, I'm going!' Rick Halliday snarled. 'But you're making a big mistake. She's the trouble. Not me!'

Paul Lamarr was unmoved. Lloyd Rivers gesticulated despair as Rick Halliday tramped away.

'Where do we go from here? You saw what we shot just then. She might as well have been a wet rag for all the emotion she showed. It ruins what could have been . . .'

'We get another man.'

Paul Lamarr's pronouncement sparked a tirade of protest from his sister. 'Another man! Are you mad, Paul? It takes time to get another man. And more time to set all this up again. Two days' shooting, you said. And who's to say Miss Childe won't object to the next man, and the next? You can't keep on with this obsessive whim of yours. To make it open-ended is sheer pigheadedness. I say she's had her chance. You've used up your budget. It finishes here!'

'Kristen has a valid point, Paul.'

He swung around to face his mother. 'You saw the film last night. It's worth going on.'

'I wouldn't like to throw this one away,' Lloyd Rivers spoke up earnestly. 'I could fit another shoot into my schedule in a fortnight's time.'

'A fortnight! Out of the question!' Kristen Delaney snapped. 'Even you can't justify gambling that far, Paul.'

He turned sharply to Lloyd Rivers. 'Can you shoot it differently? Minimising the man's role. I know he has to be there but the emphasis was always on Eve. I don't think we'd lose much if the emphasis is even more on her. Providing he's reasonably well-built he could be anyone.'

'Like more of a prop than a player,' came the eager retort. 'Yes, it can be done. But you'd better choose someone fast if it's to be done this evening. The light won't last forever.'

Paul Lamarr wheeled on Eve. 'It's up to you. Look around and pick a man.'

'So now we're down to amateur dramatics,' his sister sneered. 'If she can't co-operate with a professional actor then——'

'Shut up, Kristen! Eve ... this is your only chance.'

Eve had barely taken in the argument which had whirled around her. Once the abominable Rick Halliday had been removed she had sunk into a dull stupor, too sickened to care what was decided. She did not care about the film, the future, or her career. The last two days had been a nightmare of churning emotions and she only wanted to be released from any continuation of it.

She did not want another chance. Another chance meant dredging around her soul for more feeling and she was all used up. Worn out. Soul-weary. She stared at Paul Lamarr, her eyes pained with the burden he had laid on her.

'Come on, Eve ... choose,' he urged insistently.

Her mind sought frantically for an escape. And found one. The choice which Paul Lamarr would never accept. 'I'll do it with you.'

CHAPTER NINE

THE stunned silence was broken by a high-pitched laugh which ended in a gurgle of derision. Kristen Delaney was amused. Her brother wasn't.

'For God's sake, don't be absurd! We haven't time.'

His curt impatience only served to reassure Eve that this was indeed the best retreat open to her. 'I'll do it with you or not at all,' she stated decisively.

'An ultimatum! Your star is not very accommodating, Paul, but since this is your private little gamble, why don't you accommodate her?' Kristen jeered.

He ignored his sister. 'Be reasonable, Eve. Don't forget your career. This is make or break time!'

His words no longer had the power to stir the heavy pall of apathy around Eve's heart. She remained silent.

Her passive resistance angered him into a sharp gesture of frustration. He spoke with uncontrolled harshness. 'Then that's an end to it if you won't change your mind!'

Her only response was to sag with relief. He had released her. She could leave.

'Paul . . .' Margot Lamarr's voice slid into the impasse with all its imposing authority. '. . . we have a large investment in this commercial. In business terms, we are now in a position where we lose everything . . . or take the one possible course which might show us a profit. If Miss Childe can do it with you the Company wins.'

Alarm shrieked through Eve's nerves as she realised that Paul Lamarr was considering his mother's advice. He could not. Surely he would not.

'Rivers, have the angles worked out before I return. I'm going to change my clothes.'

A broad grin lightened the director's face. 'Yessir!' Instantly he was off, shouting orders and wildly gesticulating.

'Paul, you're not going to demean yourself by . . .' Kristen's disbelieving voice petered out as her brother strode up the beach towards the log-cabin.

Eve could not believe it either. She had been so sure he would refuse. Despair compressed her heart into a small heavy lump. How could she do it with him? She had thrown down the gauntlet, so confident that he would not pick it up. Now there was no avoiding the inevitable result. If only he had not been prompted by his mother. Eve cast a resentful look at Margot Lamarr and caught a gleam of—what was it—heightened watchfulness? Did the old lady know that Eve's gambit had been a bluff? That she had not anticipated being taken up on it?

'Come, Kristen,' she said in her not-to-be-ignored tone. 'We shall withdraw to the sidelines and leave Miss Childe to compose herself for this crucial scene—now that she has the partner of her choice.'

A painful surge of blood burnt into Eve's cheeks. There had never really been a choice. She had come to this beach and he had been here. A stranger. Her lover. The man who had shown her what it was to be a woman. He had taken her along new pathways, opened wonderful doors and led her into a new dimension of feeling. He had been a partner in a deeper sense than she had believed possible. And yes! If the clock was turned backwards she would not wish for it to be anyone else, and if the choice was hers again, she would never have left him.

But he had shed the mantle of lover, partner, understanding friend. The sharing had stopped on this beach and now she had to play out a travesty of what they had known together. He would be with her and yet not with her, acting from business necessity, forced into a partnership he did not want, a partnership from which he recoiled.

'Eve! Over here!'

Lloyd Rivers was summoning her. She forced herself to respond. The film-director was bubbling with confident enthusiasm.

'We'll do it, by God! We'll have it in the can tonight, come hell or high water. A man waits a lifetime for something like this, so don't let me down now, Eve. You've got your man. For one bloody awful minute I thought we'd had it. Thank God for the old lady! There's a woman with a business head on her shoulders. Didn't get where she is on airs and graces. A real tiger, that one!'

Lion. Lioness. Queen of the jungle, Eve

mentally corrected him, wishing fiercely that she had never come into the old lady's stamping ground.

Lloyd Rivers drew breath and plunged down to business. 'Now when Lamarr gets down here we'll have a quick run-through of the actions. You do exactly what we've rehearsed. The camera will catch you three-quarter on as you run back to him and change to full-face as he lifts you up. Only Lamarr's back view will be in the picture. Understand?'

She nodded.

'That means the whole focus is on you, Eve, so now is the time to produce everything. Give me the whole works and you'll be a star everyone'll want to see.' He glanced over her shoulder. 'Ah, there's Lamarr coming now. I'll go up and brief him.'

He hurried off and Eve's gaze was irresistibly drawn to the man who was approaching. Paul Lamarr was dressed in the same clothes he had worn that day so many weeks ago, the Tee-shirt emphasising the powerful breadth of his chest, workmanlike jeans rolled up to the muscular calves of his legs.

Memories shivered over her skin and pumped a frightening rhythm through her veins. She grasped desperately for the dignity of self-control but control was a will-o'-the-wisp, evading her completely when Paul Lamarr took up the position directed by Lloyd Rivers. He was so close, barely centimetres away. And in a matter of moments there would be no space between them.

Lloyd Rivers said the fateful words. 'Now to

start, you have to hold Eve so that her feet do not touch the sand. Once she curls her arms around your neck you let her slide down. When her feet hit the sand you let her go and she'll push into the dance routine. Okay, let's try it.'

She could not look at him. Her heart was beating like a drum gone mad. He lifted her and pinned her against his heart, the heart which had once beat in joyous unison with hers. She pressed her hands against his shoulders, keeping her eyes determinedly shut as her body trembled its treachery.

The first touch of his mouth was like an electric shock. She jerked her head back, her eyes wide open in alarm as nervous tremors shook her even more visibly. Instinctively her fingers strained against his strength in a vain attempt to halt the chaos he was provoking.

Dark eyes mocked the fear in hers. 'Aren't we supposed to be kissing?'

'Ah, well, um,' Lloyd Rivers waffled in his beard.

'There's no need to change the script,' came the curt comment.

Action followed on the words before Eve had time to voice a protest. One arm easily supported her as the other hand slid up and held her head steady. Warm, sensuous lips closed over hers, teasing, tantalising, creating havoc with her defensive resistance, until of their own accord her hands crept up around his neck. She did not even realise he was lowering her. The seductive excitement of his kiss consumed her senses. Her head swam with dizzy warmth. Not until cold

water washed around her toes did the touch of
wet sand register. Then she tore herself out of his
embrace, a clamour of self-protective instincts
demanding that she follow the script. It provided
a respite, necessary space for the madness
coursing through her body to be halted.

'Good! Good!' Lloyd Rivers boomed approval.
'Hold it there for a minute, Eve.'

She had reached the point where she pirouetted
before running back. She glanced sharply at Paul
Lamarr. He looked calm, unmoved, as if nothing
had happened. And nothing had! Just a kiss, a
short, meaningless kiss to him. Oh God! she
thought despairingly. Had she given herself
away? Did he realise how he had shaken her?
Even now she was still trembling.

'Now, Mr Lamarr. While Eve pirouettes you
move down a couple of steps and turn so that you
won't be in profile as she returns.'

He followed Lloyd Rivers' instructions.

'Right. You saw how Halliday lifted her up
high. Do the same, then turn with her in that
position so that she's silhouetted against sky and
sea . . . like this . . . before she slides down. The
camera will follow her. Got it?'

'I think so.'

'Okay, Eve! Take it from the pirouette!'

She took a deep breath and ordered her feet to
perform their practised steps. If she managed it
right this first time, maybe there would be no
need for further rehearsals. The sooner this scene
was accomplished, the sooner she could escape
from the emotional and physical turmoil aroused
by Paul Lamarr.

He caught her securely, lifted and turned precisely as Lloyd Rivers had demonstrated. Her feet dangled against his thighs. Then she was sliding down and he watched her all the way, not with the hard, impassive eyes of Paul Lamarr, but with eyes which gleamed with intimate memories, their bodies sliding together, in his bed, in the sea, need answering need.

'Splendid!' Lloyd Rivers declared excitedly. 'We won't need to waste any more time. Move back for the start and I'll have the sand cleared ready for a take.'

He clapped his hands and roared commands. Eve was in a state of shock. She did not understand what was going on in Paul Lamarr's mind and her own was incapable of reasoning. Her eyes darted around. Any target was better than the man beside her. It jolted her even further to see that the whole camp had gathered to watch. Paul Lamarr's involvement had obviously stirred a lively curiosity.

Lloyd Rivers demanded a retreat and the onlookers moved back out of range of the cameras but the heightened interest made Eve painfully self-conscious.

'Block them out.'

She glanced up, startled by the strained tone of the command. This was not the Paul Lamarr she was accustomed to seeing. This was the man who had loved her. His hand cupped her cheek, a gentle touch which awakened poignant memories.

'Pretend we're alone. Remember the feeling you had with me then. Give it back to me, Eve. Just this once.'

His voice had dropped to a husky murmur and there was a deep yearning in his eyes, a hunger which grew and enveloped her in its need to be fed.

'Why? For a film?' she choked out, not quite believing what she saw and voicing the harsh cynicism which he had taught her.

'A man can dream,' he said enigmatically, and the need became more tangible as his arms took her prisoner and he pressed the dominance of his body on to hers. 'You were a beautiful dream, Eve. It might be madness but I want to live that dream again. If it only lasts a few seconds, let me feel what we once had together.'

Her heart gave a great leap of hope. 'Then . . . then it did mean something to you. It wasn't just a . . .'

'Action!'

The words she had tried to voice withered under the fire of his desire, a fire which simultaneously burst through Eve's veins. Somehow she remembered to press her hands against his shoulders as his mouth claimed hers. Then he was lifting her, moulding her body to his, and her hands rushed around his neck, fingers thrusting into the thick hair, urgently pleading for the passion she had known with him, only with him. And it was there, exploding between them, in them, body calling to body with all the craving for fulfilment, for the appeasement of lonely, aching need. An exultant joy sprang alive and bloomed in all the empty places.

'Eve!' A hoarse murmur.

'Yes.' A breath of surrender.

Conflict ... torment ... desire in his eyes. 'Eve, you must go. Go and come back to me.'

Her feet were on the sand. She remembered what she had to do. It would only take a few moments. She danced away, flying with happiness, free of the darkness, free to love and be loved. She pirouetted with the sheer joy of being alive, brilliantly beautifully alive.

His arms were stretched out to her, wanting her back. She ran with the ethereal lightness of thistledown and he lifted her high, high, wheeling, and she arched her body against the sky in ecstatic delight, offering it as her gift to him. And slowly, melting with each moment of anticipation he gathered her down to a kiss which branded her his, a fierce claim of possession, burning into her soul, taking all she had to give. And she gave unstintingly, wanting, inviting, needing the ultimate sharing which would seal their union.

Then unbelievably he was withdrawing. His head lifted. Hard fingers dragged her apart from him. She clung on, bewildered by the abrupt severance. Firmly he took her hands and pulled them down to her side. Only then did the alien sound of applause clap into her ears, shocking her back to reality.

She stared around her, appalled by the number of witnesses. Grinning faces seemed to leer at her. They had seen. They all knew what she felt for Paul Lamarr. She shrank closer to him, instinctively seeking his protection. Lloyd Rivers was almost upon them. The director was flapping his arms with excitement.

'Thank you, Mr Lamarr,' he rolled out with relish, then lifted his hands to heaven. 'And praise be to whatever artistic muse it is which smiles upon us tonight. We have that finale locked up tight and I promise you both that I, and only I, shall edit that film with hands of reverence. Eve, you were magnificent. Mag-nificent! A privilege to watch you my dear, dear girl.'

He patted his paunch with smug self-indulgence. 'Ah, what an advertisement this'll be! Not only for your perfume, Mr Lamarr, but for Eve, for me, for the art of film-making. An achievement, by God! A shining jewel among the old, trite formulas. No cup of tea at this commercial! They'll be calling in people to watch the box, eyes drinking in the beauty of it. Grand stuff! Grand stuff! Well worth your trouble, Mr Lamarr. A generous gesture standing in for us. Yessir. And well done too.'

'Thank you, Rivers, but of course, Miss Childe is the star,' he said with an emphasis which held no pleasure in its tone.

Before she could even send him a questioning glance, Eve was clasped roundly to a swelling paunch, then held at arm's length as the film-director voiced his elation in even more grandiloquent terms.

'And what a star! Such feeling! Such expression! My dear you were utterly, utterly superb. I thank you from the depths of my artistic soul. And I shall do you justice,' he concluded with a bow which had all the flourish of a maestro.

'You're very kind,' Eve muttered, hopelessly embarrassed by the fulsome praise. It was totally undeserved. She had not acted. The film's requirements had been the last thing on her mind. If Paul had not prompted her ... she glanced back shyly, her eyes aglow with the warmth of loving.

He was not there. He had gone. A sudden chill swept her heart until she caught sight of him near the closest camera-crew. He was speaking to John Lindsey. Again she became conscious of the large number of spectators. This was no place for private conversation, but she wished he had waited for her. Perhaps he would take her home. Her work here was over. They could go together. There was so much to say, explain, satisfy.

Nan Perkins was coming forward, a beaming smile on her face. 'Well done, Eve. I'm so glad it all worked out. I sure didn't want to see those costumes wasted.'

'Great costumes!' Lloyd Rivers chimed in, clearly in the mood to lavish praise on everyone.

Paul Lamarr was moving over to his mother. He said a few words to her, nodded as she replied, then without even a glance in Eve's direction, he set off up the beach towards the cabin.

'Eve?' Nan's voice, curiously inquiring.

'Pardon?'

'I was suggesting that you come up to the caravan and change.'

'Oh!' Eve tried to collect her wits. Of course Paul Lamarr was going to change back into his business suit. She had to get out of this costume also. 'Come on then.'

If Nan had not been accompanying her, Eve

would have sprinted across the sand. As it was the other girl protested her hurry. Eve was too consumed with a sense of urgency to care what anyone thought. Her hands were reaching for the back fastenings of the dress as the caravan door closed.

'Hold on! I'll do it,' Nan insisted.

No sooner had Eve stepped out of the dress than she was thrusting her arms into the beach-coat. She was at the door again before Nan stopped her.

'Don't you want me to remove that make-up? It could be tricky.'

'Yes. Yes, of course. Sorry.' Eve forced herself to sit down. 'Please hurry, Nan,' she said anxiously as the other woman wasted precious time in hanging up the dress.

'You've got me almost out of breath as it is. What's the rush? We won't be pulling up stakes here for another hour or so.'

'I just want to . . . to get back to normal.'

Nan sighed and set about creaming Eve's face. 'I don't know. You're a funny one, Eve. Are you always so uptight? Not once have I seen you relaxed. Except when you were asleep. And then it only took a few seconds of consciousness for you to be drum-tight with tension again. You ought to take up yoga. Good for the body. Good for the mind.'

The advice fell on deaf ears. Eve's mind was racing, feverishly trying to hurdle the doubts which had suddenly grown out of her anxiety.

Surely he could not switch passion on and off, as if it had never been. Yet he had put her aside so abruptly at the end. And he had moved off without one personal word to her. How could he go like that? The feeling had been mutual, a deep, urgent reaching for each other. He had to be waiting for her out there. He had to be.

Yet there had been room in his mind for the film. His kiss had completely swept it from hers. He had not forgotten where he was and what they were supposed to be doing. When the cameras had stopped rolling ... no ... no! her brain screamed. It couldn't be so. He could not have aroused her emotion with such cynical delibera-tion. Not just for a film. He had wanted her. Really wanted her. As it had been on the beach that afternoon so long ago, the sweet sense of utter belonging. He could not turn his back on that.

But she had, Eve reminded herself painfully. He had asked her to stay and she had gone. Gone for a whole lot of muddled up reasons and with a cutting rejection on her lips. A beautiful dream. That's what he'd said. He did not believe it could last. Last for him? Or for her? she had to speak to him. She had to know.

'That'll do!' She sprang up from the chair, almost knocking it over in her haste.

'There's still some glitter . . .'

Eve was already stumbling down the caravan steps, her pulse hammering out its panic. The door of the log-cabin was opening. Paul Lamarr came out. He glanced towards her. Eve held her breath. His eyes met hers but there was no spark of recognition, acknowledgement, anything personal. Just darkness. Like ashes whose flame had been thoroughly extinguished. Dead.

The hard mask of authority stamped his face, cold, ruthless, impenetrable. The distance between them was not only physical. He had removed himself from her, mentally and emotionally. If somewhere inside him there beat a soft spot of vulnerability, it did not show. He was Paul Lamarr. Head of the Company.

Eve could not bring herself to speak. She did not have the strength to batter at the wall between them. It was too high, too formidable, and she was not even sure if there was a vulnerable spot.

He gave her a distant little nod, walked straight to the BMW which had been parked next to the Land-Rover, and drove away. She watched until it disappeared behind the thick scrub.

A beautiful dream. A fantasy. Locked into film but its substance thrown away. The man on the beach was lost to her forever.

CHAPTER TEN

DEAR Miss Childe,

Margot Lamarr requests your attendance at a private screening of the promotion film for Fantasy perfume. It is to be held in the Conference Room of the Lamarr building at 5.00 p.m. this Friday, 23rd March.

Refreshments will be served and you are invited to bring a guest if you so wish.

Yours sincerely,
John Lindsey.

'Well?'

The expectant ring in her mother's voice grated on Eve's ears. Marion Childe had thrust the letter into her daughter's hands, demanding that it be opened immediately. The Lamarr emblem on the envelope had obviously given rise to feverish speculation while Eve had been out shopping.

'Nothing definite,' Eve replied flatly.

'It must be something. They wouldn't write for nothing,' her mother insisted.

Marion Childe's fingers were fidgeting. Eve sighed and passed her the letter. There would be no peace until her mother had read it, and probably no peace afterwards. Until a contract was offered or refused by the Lamarr Corporation her mother would endlessly nag on the subject.

Ever since she had returned from the beach, Eve had lived in an emotional limbo, unable to stir herself to excitement or enthusiasm about anything. The future was a dull, grey, amorphous blob and she did not want to think about it, let alone discuss plans for it. Her mother had been frustrated by Eve's reluctance to talk about the filming. She had kept digging for more details, questioning and speculating on the answers until Eve had completely closed up, refusing to speak about it any more.

'But this is marvellous, Eve!' Marion Childe's eyes glowed with excitement. 'They wouldn't bother showing a film they're not interested in. And they wouldn't invite you unless they intended to sign you up. Read between the lines. You've got it!'

'There's no commitment, Mum. Don't get carried away. It's only an invitation.'

'But the invitation speaks for itself. I don't know how you can be so cool about it, Eve. Think of what it can mean to you.' Her eyes glowed even more brightly. 'Oh, I can't wait until Friday! To see your work and meet Margot Lamarr. It'll be——'

'I don't want you to go, Mum.'

Shock and hurt chased across Marion Childe's face. 'Eve, you can't mean that. The letter says you can bring a guest.'

Eve sighed. 'To tell you the truth, I'm not sure I'll sign a contract, even if I'm offered one. I couldn't do a job like that again.' To her intense mortification tears filled her eyes and trickled down her cheeks. She hurriedly dashed them away but more kept coming.

'Eve . . .' The hurt bewilderment on Marion Childe's face suddenly cracked and the mother in her rushed to comfort. She hugged her daughter close, patting her back, stroking her hair, murmuring soothing words as deep, heart-wrenching sobs came tumbling out in uncontrolled bursts.

Eve finally dragged herself away, ashamed of her breakdown and apologising in a string of incoherent words. Marion Childe led her into the living-room, sat her down on the sofa and took her hands, rubbing them in gentle sympathy.

'Eve, you've locked me out ever since the break-up with Simon,' she began tentatively.

Eve shook her head. 'You wouldn't listen.'

'I'm sorry. I thought I knew what was best for you. I don't know what's going on any more,' she admitted despondently. 'You've insisted on going out on your own and maybe I have been too . . . too domineering in the past, but you didn't have any direction of your own, Eve. You needed looking after. You looked to me to make decisions.'

She dragged in a deep breath and plunged on. 'Now you want to make your own decisions. I have to accept that. But please, can't we talk about them? It's a very lonely place out there and I want to help. You may not think I've been a good mother but I do love you, Eve, and I care very, very much, what happens to you. Please don't lock me out.'

'Oh, Mum, I don't know what I want,' Eve poured out in a rush, then gave a shaky little smile. 'But it has been very lonely these last few weeks.'

'Why don't you want me to go on Friday, Eve?' her mother asked softly, and hurt was still there, mixed with a need to understand.

'It's . . . you'll see . . .' How to explain that she felt too embarrassed by the naked emotion which would be on show. Eve sighed. 'You can come, but please don't push anything, Mum. I'm not sure I want to have any further connection with the Lamarrs. They demand too much.'

Her mother frowned. 'What do you mean?'

'All they care about is selling their product,' she said bitterly.

'But, Eve. That's business.'

The green eyes became even more bleak. 'I know. But I didn't like being a pawn in a power-game, prodded and fought over and knocked aside when I'd been used to give them what they wanted.'

'But it works both ways, dear. You use them to get what you want. You shouldn't take it so personally.'

But it was personal. Terribly personal. Only Eve could not bring herself to explain that. It hurt too much. 'You're probably right, Mum. It's just that I can't cope with it.'

'Will you let me help? I can stand between you and the Lamarrs, Eve. What you need is an agent to protect you,' her mother said eagerly.

'Mum, don't push. Please just let it ride for now. Wait until Friday and I'll see how I feel about it after the film is shown.'

For once Marion Childe did not pursue her

own point of view. She went out of her way to
pamper Eve, cooking tasty meals to tempt her
appetite, buying tickets for a musical which had
won acclaim on Broadway and had just opened in
Sydney, making bright conversation and being
generally indulgent towards her daughter. Eve
appreciated her mother's efforts. There was still a
large gap in their understanding but that was not
something that could easily be bridged. Their
outlooks on life were too diverse but at least there
was sympathetic communication and Eve's loneli-
ness was eased.

Friday came and as the day wore on Eve
became more silent and tense. Her mother tried
to fuss her into wearing something the Lamarr
people had not seen but Eve chose the pink and
green dress she had worn to the interview with
Margot Lamarr. It gave her a perverse satisfaction
to wear a bra underneath it. No one was going to
tell her to take it off this time, Eve thought
grimly. Nor was she going to be intimated by any
of the Lamarrs.

She applied a subtle make-up, designed more
to disguise her pallor and the slight shadows
under her eyes than to enhance her natural
beauty, but it served both purposes. She left her
hair in its natural curls. It was easier than going
to a hairdresser for a more formal style. She even
dabbed on the Fantasy perfume which Margot
Lamarr had given her. The scent was fresh and
oddly definable. It made one want to smell it
again and again. No doubt it would sell well, Eve
thought bitterly.

Marion Childe had dressed with her usual,

impeccable taste. Her cream silk suit was teamed
with a yellow and cream blouse in a soft crêpe de
chine. She looked very elegant with her upswept
blonde hair and carefully subdued make-up and
she smiled with genuine pleasure when Eve told
her so.

They arrived at the Lamarr building with five
minutes to spare. John Lindsey met them in the
lobby and escorted them up to the Conference
Room, answering Marion Childe's questions
along the way with his easy charm. He ushered
them into a room which already seemed full of
people. Eve recognised some faces but by no
means all. The gathering suddenly parted and
Margot Lamarr swept down the room towards
them with all the stateliness of a queen.

'My dear Miss Childe, a pleasure to have you
with us again. And this is . . .'

'My mother, Mrs Marion Childe.'

'Indeed? You're very welcome, Mrs Childe.
This is a gathering of the people who have been
involved in the production of our new perfume,
from laboratory to publicity. I will not waste time
in introducing you now. I'm sure you're as
impatient to see the finished film as everyone else
is. Come, sit with me.'

It had been an extremely courteous greeting
and Eve smiled at the gratified look on her
mother's face. There was an excited hum around
the room as they moved forward. Those people
standing quickly seated themselves. Eve saw Paul
Lamarr lead an obviously pregnant lady to an
armchair. Her heart gave a sickening lurch and
she looked away.

Kristen Delaney gave Eve a thin smile from across the room. She was talking to Lloyd Rivers who beamed with bonhomie. Nan Perkins gave a little wave. Other faces seemed to peer curiously at her. Eve was glad to sit down in the front row of seats. Even though she was placed next to Margot Lamarr, at least she had her back to the crowd. Eve fixed her gaze on the large screen which dominated the end wall. She wished it was smaller, wished even more fiercely that she had not come at all. To see what was going to be shown could only give her pain.

The lights went out. The darkness was comforting. The few murmurs died into an expectant hush. The screen flashed blue. Black and gold lettering boldly spelled out:

LAMARR
presents
FANTASY

Then instantly there was the sound of the sea and behind it a flute, beginning a haunting melody. The sea rolled out of the blueness on the screen, shimmering into a horizon of glorious colour. The camera followed the fading hues around the sky until suddenly there was Eve on the beach with her bag of shells.

Her first instinct was to shut her eyes but there was a dreadful fascination in watching the emotional play of expression on the face up there on the screen, and the emotion seemed to be intensified by the flute in the background, trilling, swooping, interpreting every feeling with its purity of sound.

The sea-haze which was used for the transition from girl to mermaid was brilliantly done, a waver of misty colour accompanied by one long, drawn-out note from the flute. The editing had been masterly. It was impossible to tell where Paul Lamarr had taken over from Rick Halliday.

Eve cringed as the focus fastened on her face in the last sequence. It was all there, the joy, the excitement, the ecstasy of loving and being loved, the exquisite anticipation of fulfilment. And if it wasn't plain enough the music told the story, rising and rising in an exultant crescendo. Mercifully the film ended on a shot of the Fantasy shell around her neck as she slid down to the last embrace. If it had included the final kiss she would have died of embarrassment. The screen blacked out. The lights were switched on. Eve squirmed in the ensuing silence.

'Am I or am I not a genius?' Lloyd Rivers demanded in fulsome tones.

Somebody laughed and then applause broke out, loud, enthusiastic, almost deafening applause. Lloyd Rivers swaggered up to Eve, pulled her on to her feet and held up a hand for quiet.

'You're right! I am most certainly a genius,' he declared patting his stomach with affection before throwing out his hand in a sweeping gesture. 'But I present to you a star who could rival the young Ingrid Bergman . . . if she could cure herself of being a director's nightmare.'

More laughter and even louder applause. Eve blushed furiously. The film-director would not let her go. He had centre-stage and he was not about to give it up.

'And let me say, if that doesn't sell your Fantasy perfume, nothing will. I thank you all for your contribution to my art.'

A mood of happy triumph hung over the following uproar. Eve took the opportunity to slide down into her seat as John Lindsey called the room to order.

'I believe Mrs Lamarr would like to say a few words.'

The old lady stood and the hush was instant.

'I congratulate all of you who have worked on this project to bring it to fruition. The Lamarr name is enhanced by this new perfume, the best I think we have ever produced. It was worthy of a new concept in publicity and I congratulate my son on his imaginative idea, and his foresight in selecting Miss Childe to play the starring role.'

Eve darted a glance at Paul Lamarr who had not moved from the side of the pregnant lady. His eyes were hooded and his face could have been granite for all the expression it showed. Nothing had changed. She had not expected it to but the pain in her heart stabbed a little deeper. Not even a graphic reminder of what they had shared could pierce his inflexible will.

'I congratulate Mr Rivers,' a dry little smile was bestowed on him, 'on his genius. The camera-work and editing was indeed brilliant.' A warmer smile was directed at the pregnant lady. 'I thank Mrs Knight, perhaps better known to the public as the song-writer, Jenny Ross, who very graciously consented to compose the music which so beautifully expresses the mood of the film.'

There was a stir of interest, a craning of necks to see the woman whose name conjured up so many memorable songs. Eve now understood why Paul Lamarr had been so attentive. Jenny Ross was a guest of very special note. A mere model paled in comparison. She sighed and wished once more that she had not come.

Margot Lamarr looked directly at Eve as she continued. 'As you all know, it has been company policy for many years to use established stars for publicising our products. This time we gambled with Miss Childe. Some of us held grave doubts about her ability to project the mood we envisaged, but I don't think any of us anticipated the sheer, poignant beauty of a performance which will be memorable for many years to come. It is our incredibly good fortune that for some time at least, she will be spoken of as the Lamarr Fantasy girl.'

Eve was too stunned to resist when Margot Lamarr took her hand and drew her to her feet again. There was a nerve-tingling silence. Everyone was staring at her and she suddenly realised they were seeing her, not as the woman who stood before them, but as the girl on the screen. Something like a collective sigh ran around the room. Eve writhed in self-conscious agony. This was far worse than applause. Instinctively her eyes sought Paul Lamarr's and this time he too, was looking at her.

It was for you, only for you. Don't you know that? she cried silently. He closed his eyes and bowed his head as if he did not want to receive her message.

Margot Lamarr concluded her speech. 'I now invite you all to stay and celebrate the culmination of your work with the refreshments which are being wheeled in.'

It was a signal for more clapping and a general hubbub followed as people rose to their feet. Eve was grateful to everyone who stood. It made her feel less conspicuous. The light pressure on her hand signalled that Margot Lamarr had not yet finished with her. She turned to the old lady, wary of any personal talk.

'A contract has been drawn up, Miss Childe. It only awaits your consideration and subsequently your signature. John Lindsey will be fixing an appointment with you before you leave this evening. I hope it gives you satisfaction.'

'I'll consider it, Mrs Lamarr,' Eve said quietly.

The black eyes sharply probed Eve's guard but her defences were firmly in place. She was not going to be drawn into a commitment here and now.

Margot Lamarr switched her gaze to Marion Childe who was rising to her feet in a slightly dazed fashion. 'You must be very proud of your daughter, Mrs Childe.'

Marion Childe shook her head as if to clear it. 'I don't know what to say. I never imagined . . .' She looked at her daughter in obvious wonderment. 'Eve, you were just amazing. I never realised that you could act so expressively.'

'Yet your daughter stated flatly that she is not an actress,' Margot Lamarr remarked with an oddly questioning look at Eve. 'It was, one might say, an illuminating performance, and one which,

perhaps, carries its own reward. Ah, Kristen.'
She turned to her own daughter who had
descended on them with a forced courtesy on her
face. 'This is Mrs Childe, Eve's mother. My
daughter, Kristen Delaney.'

'How do you do?' Marion Childe murmured
weakly, still rather overwhelmed by the occasion.

Kristen Delaney inclined her head in regal
fashion before turning to Eve. 'What a surprise
package you turned out to be, Miss Childe! But
then, there's nothing like having the advantage of
inside knowledge and Paul certainly had that,
didn't he? Lloyd Rivers has just been telling me
how . . .'

Margot Lamarr interrupted with all the
smoothness of a very sharp knife. 'Kristen, sour
grapes never go down well.' Then she smiled, the
lioness baring her teeth. 'Have a glass of
champagne. It's much more suited to the
occasion.'

A waiter had arrived with a tray of drinks.
Behind him came Paul Lamarr and another man,
Robert Knight, who was not only Jenny Ross's
husband but a producer for television. Lloyd
Rivers descended once again. John Lindsey and
Nan Perkins joined the cluster of people. Toasts
were made, congratulations passed around, but
not a word from Paul Lamarr. Eve smiled and
nodded like an automaton, only vaguely conscious
of what was being said. She was intensely aware
of Paul Lamarr's silence. She willed him to say
something, anything, open up even the most
tenuous thread of communication.

He was watching her with a chillingly detached

air. Robert Knight expressed interest in contact-
ing her agent. Marion Childe stated that she was
managing her daughter's career. Lloyd Rivers
expounded on Eve's future in glowing terms and
her mother lapped it up, adding her own
ambitious comments.

Career. Career. Career. A sledgehammer striking at the wedge between them, driving Paul
Lamarr further away. His withdrawal was almost
tangible. Eve wanted to reach out, stop him,
scream that a career had no meaning to her. What
she had shown him up there on the screen . . .
that was the only reality. She did not want the
bright lights, only the warmth of his love.

Desperation overrode pride. She looked at him
with all the torment of need in her expressive
green eyes. There was one startled flicker of
response before he wrenched his gaze away, his
face stiff with rejection. He muttered a couple of
words to his mother and smoothly extracted
himself from the group around Eve. He skirted
the crowd with quick, purposeful strides and left
the room.

John Lindsey touched her arm and said
something about a contract. Eve's heart was
beating an agonised protest, pleading for, demanding one last chance. Her feet followed its
dictate, taking her past people, automatically
choosing Paul Lamarr's path, quickening with
urgency as she reached the doorway.

The corridor outside was empty. She ran
around the corner to the bank of lifts. The
indicator showed one going down. She jabbed at
other buttons. She had to catch him. Tell him.

Make him listen. Tears of frustration filled her
eyes as the steel doors remained shut.

'Eve! Wait!'

She turned to John Lindsey in a frenzy of
impatience. 'I don't want your contract,' she
hurled at him. Her hands reached feverishly for
the buttons again.

'Stop her, John!'

Restraining hands caught her shoulders as the
elevator doors opened.

'Let me go! I have to go!' Eve sobbed
frantically.

'Mrs Lamarr?'

Heels clicking on the corridor. 'Thank you. I
won't need you any more.'

Surprise held Eve rooted to the spot for a
moment. Then she realised she was free. She
rushed into the lift and slammed her hand on the
DOWN button. The doors rolled shut but not
before Margot Lamarr had stepped into the
compartment.

The old lady eyed Eve with age-old experience.
'Do you know what you're doing?'

'I don't care. I don't care about a career,' Eve
flung at her, her own eyes darting desperately to
the flashing numbers. Fourth floor . . . third . . .
the lift was crawling down. Oh God! Make it go
faster, she begged.

'My dear, one should always keep options
open. The contract will still be waiting for you on
Monday if you change your mind.'

'I won't change it.' Second floor. Come on.
Come on, she screamed silently.

'No. I don't think you will. By the way, if it

means anything to you, he told me he was going fishing.'

Going fishing. Eve's heart swelled with emotion. She turned to the old lady, tears of relief trickling down her cheeks. 'I must go. I love him,' she whispered.

Margot Lamarr gave a tired little smile. 'I'll tell your mother where you've gone.'

Eve's smile was wobbly. 'Thank you.'

The lift doors opened on to the lobby. Eve walked out, hope soaring high as her mind and heart leapt ahead to the man on the beach.

CHAPTER ELEVEN

No light winked at her from the cabin. Panic pressed her foot down on the accelerator. The car leapt forward, almost bouncing out of control on the rutted track. He had to be there. Had to be. The headlights picked out the Land-Rover by the side of the cabin and relief coursed through her veins. He was there. She brought her car to a screeching halt, then sat for a few moments, gathering her courage into determined purpose. He was not going to turn her away. She would not let him.

Even so her steps grew hesitant as she approached the cabin. It took every bit of her will-power to push open the door and walk inside. The darkness held no sound. The room felt empty. She forced herself to speak.

'Paul? Where are you?'

No answer.

The beach. He would be on the beach. She kicked out of her sandals and rolled off her panti-hose, tossing them on the nearest chair. Bare-footed and with her heart pumping out its urgency she ran outside. Her eyes immediately caught the dark silhouette at the water's edge. She could not tell if he was turned towards her or the sea. He stood motionless. She kept running, the heavy sand underfoot slowing her progress but not until she could see that he was facing her did she falter to a walk.

Still he did not move. Not one step towards
her. He could have been a statue but for the dark
glitter of his eyes. His hands were thrust into the
pockets of a windcheater, his head thrown back a
little at a proud, forbidding angle.

Eve stopped and caught her breath. His stance
held no invitation yet she sensed that he was
waiting, wanting her to speak. She swallowed and
chose her words carefully, reaching back to a time
of beautiful harmony.

'Can I . . . can I stay with you?'

His chin lowered sharply and she heard his
breath hiss out as if he had held it for a long time.
Tension shrieked around her nerves as she waited
for his answer.

'If you want to.'

Still he made no move towards her. Only the
four soft words, barely audible above the sound
of the sea. Then slowly he drew one hand from a
pocket and held it out to her. She took it as one
would a life-line, her fingers winding around his
in a tight grip. There was a look of disbelief in his
eyes. Eve smiled assurance, but it was a
tremulous smile, affected by too many uncertainties.

'Let's walk,' he suggested gruffly.

It was enough to begin with. To be beside him,
arm brushing arm, in step together, knowing he
accepted her presence. Dying waves curled
around their feet just as they had so many weeks
ago. The innocence had been lost and there was
much pain to be appeased, but it was a beginning.
A shell rolled against her foot and she paused to
pick it up.

'Don't!'

The sharp command stabbed out, a cry of torment. She straightened instantly, looking up at him with anxious eyes. He shook his head and dragged in a deep breath.

'Eve, I don't want a fantasy. I've tramped this beach too many times, wanting you to come back. When you ran down to me it was like a dream come true, but——'

She placed a silencing hand on his lips. 'No buts. I'm not a dream. I'm here. Feel me. Love me as you did before. I want you to.' She pressed her body close, wound her arms around his neck and lifted her mouth to his. 'I love you, I want you, I need you,' she murmured in a litany of longing.

He groaned, a deep, primitive sound which she smothered with her kiss. Then his arms were around her, crushing her against him as he took her offering with passionate hunger. His hands moved over her in restless possession, thighs, hips, waist, back, hair, needing to confirm her reality. She savoured every touch, wanting more and more.

'Let's go up to the cabin,' she whispered.

He seemed reluctant to move.

'Here then. It doesn't matter where.'

She slid out of his hold and stripped in front of him, dropping her clothes carelessly on the sand, inviting his desire with every sensuous move of her body. She felt free, uninhibited and exultant that he could not tear his eyes away from her. Her pulse beat faster and faster but she knew the race was almost won. He wanted her every bit as

much as she wanted him. Surrender was just a
breath away. She unzipped his windcheater,
pressing her naked breasts against his warm skin
and running her hands over his broad shoulders
as she pushed the restrictive material aside.

'Eve . . . not here.' Hands tightened around her
waist and dragged her back so that his gaze could
feast on her. 'My God! I want to drown in you all
night.'

Elation bubbled up into a triumphant little
laugh. 'The sea then.'

He caught her wild mood and laughed also.
'No, not the sea, my little mermaid. You're far
too much woman for a cold bed.'

'I'll race you up to the cabin.'

She had broken free of his hold and was metres
away in moments. She glanced back to see him
still standing there, a bemused grin on his face.

'Come on. There's just you and me and the
sea. Let's be free,' she sang in excitement.

He laughed, a sheer, boyish whoop of laughter,
then scooped up her clothes and gave chase. She
had almost reached the road when he dived and
caught her ankle. He cut off her shriek with his
mouth and their kiss grew in urgency. It was he
who broke it, breathing harshly as he pulled
himself up and lifted her to her feet.

'You're not a mermaid. You're a witch. Let's
get this sand off us.'

He hurried her to the cabin, led her through
the main room to the laundry. Water hissed down
from the shower. It was cold but Eve did not
care. Warm hands caressed the sand from her
body. There was no rough washing this time and

he did not jerk away when she touched him. He turned off the taps and reached over a towel. She took it from him and slowly wiped the moisture from his body, loving him with her hands and lips until he groaned and tore the towel away.

In an instant she was scooped up in his arms and held against a wildly thumping heart. She kissed the leaping pulse in his throat as he carried her to the bed, then lay with her body open to him, pulling him down on top of her.

'No. Let me look at you.'

A pale moonlight streamed through the window. Slowly his fingers traced the curves of her body, tantalising her skin with their light touch.

'You are so very beautiful,' he murmured and there was gloating pleasure in the soft tone.

He kissed her breasts, trailed his tongue down to her navel and lower, paying a devastating homage to her body. The intimate stroking set her trembling with feverish pleasure but her need to hold him, own him, be him, was far too great to savour the erotic sensations he was arousing.

'No more,' she gasped. 'I need you now.'

And he was hers. She joyfully wrapped her arms around him and lifted her body to meet his. He entered her slowly and the movement inside her was exquisite. This was no impatient thrust but the loving possession of a connoisseur intent on savouring what he owned to the fullest extent. Eve writhed on the edge of ecstasy, pleading incoherently to be taken further.

Then there was no more control. Their hearts beat in wild exultation as they abandoned themselves to each other, reaching for that peak of fulfilment where at last their bodies melted together in the liquid warmth of ultimate unity. And there they clung, physically sated yet holding on to the emotional security of their oneness, reluctant to let it end.

He rolled on to his back, carrying her with him so that her head lay over his heart. He stroked her hair, her back, long, lingering caresses which made her shiver with sensitivity.

'How long have I got, Eve?'

The flat resignation in his voice drove a needle of uncertainty into her heart. 'What do you mean?' she asked in a nervous rush.

He sighed and it was a shudder running through his body. 'One day? Two? Will you stay with me 'til Sunday night?'

She slid her hands around and under his chest, hugging him tightly to her. 'For as long as you want me,' she promised huskily. 'I don't want to ever leave you.'

She felt the sharp intake of his breath and the odd little skip of his heart. His fingers wound through her curls, absently tugging them.

'You mean this weekend. I know you're to sign the contract on Monday.' His voice was carefully stripped of emotion, too carefully. He was hiding from her.

She hauled herself into a sitting position and bent forward to look into his eyes. They were black depths of stillness, waiting, expecting nothing, just waiting. She touched his cheek in a tender caress, sending out her love through gentle finger-tips.

'I don't want a career. I told them before I followed you that I didn't want a contract. The only Lamarr girl I want to be is yours. And yours I'll be for however long you want me ... a weekend, a month, a year, all my life ... if you'll have me.'

She kissed him, using soft, persuasive lips to convince him that her offer was no transient thing but a need which could only be answered by him.

He took her head between his hands and lifted it away. 'Don't! Don't say what you don't mean, Eve.' There was emotion now. His voice was raw with it, eyes glittering with a vulnerability she had never seen before. 'I've got to know what to expect. You can have your career. I wouldn't try to take that from you. I don't know how I'll bear the separations but I'll adjust. So long as you love me like this when we're together.'

'Oh, Paul! I'll always be your love,' she assured him tenderly. 'I'm no actress. I don't even like being a model. It was something my mother pushed me into because of my looks. It was her ambition, not mine. I just went along with it because I didn't know what else to do and it pleased her. It was you who kept pushing career at me and I agreed with you out of pride. That first day in your office when you touched me, all I wanted was to feel again the magic we shared on the beach. It had nothing to do with the job.'

The struggle between belief and disbelief brought a pained tautness to his voice. 'You cannot conceive how hard it was for me to reject you that day, Eve, but you had already rejected

ne and the magic we shared to go back to your
career. I thought you could not have felt what I
felt. Otherwise you couldn't have walked away as
you did . . . right after we had made love . . . how
could you?'

She sighed and gently smoothed the lines of
pain from his forehead. 'Remember how I was
when you found me? I was terribly hurt and
disillusioned. What happened between us came
too fast on the heels of that. It really did seem
like a dream to me. It wasn't until I was back in
my real life that I understood what I had left
behind.'

'But you could have come back. You couldn't
have really believed that I'd set out to use you for
gain. I was here, every night for weeks, waiting
for you.'

The lonely yearning in his voice stabbed her
with guilt. She was ashamed of the truth but it
had to be said. 'I was frightened. I didn't know
who or what you were. I was too much of a
coward to take a blind plunge.'

His silence was ominous. His next words were
even more so, quiet, deadly words. 'But it's all
right now that I'm Paul Lamarr.'

The man she loved had suddenly been
supplanted by the cold, ruthless Paul Lamarr of
the Lamarr Corporation. Eve felt as if she had
been slapped again. She shrank away and curled
into a tight, lonely ball. The bed creaked as he
moved. She flinched from the soft touch on her
shoulder.

'It doesn't matter. I don't care why you're with
me as long as you are. Don't turn away from me,

Eve.' He curved his body around hers and gentled her stiffness with loving hands. Warm lips nuzzled the curve of neck and shoulder. 'Nothing in my whole life has equalled what I felt for you that day. Do you know what you were like? A little girl lost. I wanted to comfort you, ease your pain, give you whatever you wanted. It was a delight to see you emerge from the shadows in your mind. You were like a butterfly, climbing out of its chrysalis and spreading its wings to the sun.'

His hand cupped her breast and his voice deepened with husky longing. 'I wanted to capture and hold you but I couldn't spoil your flight. You glowed with such a special kind of joy. When you gave yourself to me, it was magic beyond my wildest dreams, like embracing all the elemental things of life and knowing they were yours. I thought I had everything a man could ever want ... But you went away.'

He sighed and it was a long, wavering breath through her hair. The desolation which had echoed in his voice brought tears to her eyes. She had no doubt now that he loved her but it still hurt that he doubted her love. She turned and slipped her arms around his neck, giving him the reassurance of her body.

'I won't leave again. Not unless you send me away. I didn't mean to hurt you, Paul. I just couldn't think straight and I didn't trust my own feelings. Don't you see how confusing it was for me? I thought I was broken-hearted over Simon's betrayal. I had believed myself in love with him. Then suddenly you had blotted him out of my mind. I couldn't understand how I could be so fickle. It was as if the whole world had turned around and I had slipped off its axis. I felt I had to climb back to reality.

'And when you turned out to be Paul Lamarr and set me up for the film, I was even more confused. I had dreamed of the man on the beach but I hated you as Paul Lamarr. I hated what you were doing to me. If there had been a viable alternative I wouldn't have gone on with it. As it was, I didn't seem to have much choice.'

'What do you mean? You could have refused.'

He was frowning. She sighed and drew a smoothing hand across his forehead. 'Didn't you know I couldn't get work?'

He shook his head, the frown cutting even deeper.

'Oh, Paul! I was just about desperate. No one wanted to use me without Simon behind the camera. We'd been a team, you see. But I couldn't go on working with him. Not after ... well, you know. Anyway he'd come around trying to tell me I was a silly fool, and Mum was backing him up, nagging at me all the time. Then the Lamarr offer came along and I kind of waved it in their faces, showing them that I could be independent. I didn't know you were behind it. I thought it was a genuine offer and it seemed my only chance to get back on my feet, all by myself. I was thrown completely off-balance when I walked into your office and saw you.'

'I didn't know,' he muttered. 'I didn't even consider such a factor.'

He rolled on to his back and lay in brooding

silence. The abrupt separation alarmed Eve. She slid a tentative hand across his chest, wanting to reinforce her presence. He caught her hand and squeezed it.

'So you felt trapped into playing the role. You didn't really want to do it,' he said with slow deliberation.

She sighed and nestled against him. 'It was either accept the job or admit failure. It sickened me that you should want to commercialise what had been very special and very personal, but I reasoned that since it had meant so little to you, I shouldn't let it mean so much to me. But it hurt, and in the end I couldn't do it ... at least, not until you stepped in and took Rick Halliday's place. I didn't mean you to, you know. It was just a way out. I thought you'd refuse.'

He cradled her more tightly. 'I've been a fool, a blind stupid fool,' he stated with a fine edge of self-contempt. 'The signs were all there if only I'd had the eyes to read them from a different slant.'

He stirred and leaned over her, eyes begging forgiveness as he tenderly brushed the curls away from her temples. 'And you had to come to me. I don't deserve you, Eve. I've been so damned full of myself, pride, ego, call it what you will ... all this time I've thought only of what I wanted.'

'That's not true,' she contradicted softly. 'You thought you were giving me the career I wanted.'

'No.' He dragged in a deep breath and let it out slowly. 'All I thought of was making you come back to me. The film had nothing to do with selling perfume or lifting you to stardom. It was only to remind you of what we had shared, make you want it again. I was too proud to beg ... at least I was until I had you in my arms for that last scene. Then I couldn't stop myself. I wanted you so badly that any crumb would do.'

'Then why did you walk away afterwards?' The remembered hurt drove a note of accusation into her voice. 'You must have known I wasn't acting, Paul.'

'Your response threw me into complete turmoil. I hadn't expected you to give yourself like that. I didn't know if you were teasing me, exulting with your power, or what. I was angry at myself for begging and angry at you for putting a career ahead of what we had together. I'd shown you how much I wanted you but I wasn't going to grovel at your feet. When I came out of the cabin and you were standing by the caravan, my damned pride insisted that you take the first step towards me. But you didn't move. You just stood there.'

'I was waiting for a signal from you,' she explained. 'I was churning ... I thought you might have done it just to get the film. It was such a turnabout. I didn't know what to think and you looked so cold and distant. Even tonight I wasn't sure. I tried to show you what I felt after the film was shown but you turned away and left.'

'I had to go. I couldn't stand another minute of hearing about your career. I knew that you wanted me, Eve. I saw it in your eyes. But I wasn't sure if I could stand being your part-time lover, always craving for more than you'd be prepared to give me. I didn't want to come second to a camera. I drove here to sort it all out in my mind.'

'And what conclusion did you come to?' she asked softly.

He smiled, a wryly tender smile. 'None. I just walked along dreaming of a girl I once knew, wishing it was possible to go back in time. Then she arrived.'

Eve teased the corners of his smile with a tracing finger. 'Were you surprised?'

He considered for a moment, then shook his head. 'It seemed like I'd been waiting for you so you came. I didn't really question it. I'd dreamed of it so often that when it happened, I felt I was still dreaming.'

'I was terrified that you would reject me,' she confessed, sure now that rejection was no longer even a remote possibility.

He grinned. 'You had a very persuasive way of sorting me out. In fact you can sort me out like that anytime you feel like it.'

Her cheeks burned at the reminder of her blatant wantonness. 'I thought action might be better than words,' she said shyly.

'Much, much better,' he agreed and kissed her very thoroughly. He came up for air and added, 'Mind you, some of those words were pretty powerful. Would you say them again?'

'What?'

'Oh, things like . . . I love you, I want you, I need you. And . . . I never want to leave you . . . The trouble was I didn't quite believe you earlier on tonight.'

The warmth in her heart flooded into her voice as she repeated what he wanted to hear.

'And you'll marry me?' he prompted softly, with a wealth of feeling which more than matched hers.

Tears of happiness filmed her eyes. 'If you want me to,' she whispered huskily.

He planted little kisses all around her face then hovered over her mouth. 'Eve, you are my love and my life. I never want to be without you again.' And his kiss demonstrated all the fervour of his declaration. It sparked the desire for more intimate possession and as their passion grew, so did their joy in each other. 'This isn't a fantasy, is it, my darling?' Paul murmured provocatively.

'No.' Eve laughed in exultation. 'No, it's real. Oh, Paul! It's beautifully, wonderfully real.'

Take 4 best-selling love stories FREE
Plus get a FREE surprise gift!

What the press says about Harlequin romance fiction...

"When it comes to romantic novels...
Harlequin is the indisputable king."
— *New York Times*

"...always with an upbeat, happy ending."
— *San Francisco Chronicle*

"Women have come to trust these
stories about contemporary people,
set in exciting foreign places."
— *Best Sellers*, New York

"The most popular reading matter of
American women today."
— *Detroit News*

"...a work of art."
— *Globe & Mail*, Toronto